Pursued By Evil

By
Cynthia M. Hickey

PublishAmerica

Baltimore

First printing

ISBN: 1-4137-2067-6
PUBLISHED BY PUBLISHAMERICA, LLLP
www.publishamerica.com
Baltimore

Printed in the United States of America

To my husband Tom
For his unfailing love, support and knowledge
So that I could do this.
Without his believing in me,
There would be no book.
And to God
For making this dream come true.

tossed Michael a little wave as he stopped at the sight of the armed men. Dylan then held Felicia tightly to his chest and kissed her tenderly on the forehead. He didn't know where Luther was, or what was happening to the people of his community, and at this moment he didn't care. He listened as his five friends issued orders and organized the people into small groups. His work was done and he laughed. He had done it. He had saved Felicia and the children and had caused the additional deaths of no one. Felicia would be pleased. He looked up into the night sky. "Thank you."

Chapter 1

"See ya later, Honey!" The old woman smiled fondly as she watched the young woman run outside, letting the screen door bang shut behind her. Felicia had called the old woman honey since she first learned to talk, mistaking the endearment the older woman called the child for the woman's name. By the time she was old enough to know the difference, the name had stuck. Honey parted the faded blue and white checked curtains and, frowning watched as the younger woman jumped into the honking pickup truck waiting outside. She sighed and turned away, back to the kitchen. How many times had she told Felicia that a properly brought up young lady shouldn't be running and slamming doors, much less jumping into trucks whose drivers didn't have the decency to come in instead of waiting outside honking. Felicia would be twenty-one tomorrow and the old woman hadn't mentally prepared her mind, or her heart, to let go of the girl she had raised from infancy.

She glanced around the old farm kitchen, taking in the battered cabinets which were painted a brilliant white, the scuffed blue speckled linoleum on the floor, the old wooden table, stained and marred, and the four-mismatched kitchen chairs. She sighed again and thought of the life that Felicia had been born into. A life of wealth and servants. Not this poor one on a lonely dirt road off a little traveled highway. She plunged her hands into a sink of hot sudsy water and dirty dishes. Somehow the mindless repetition of washing dishes always soothed her.

How would Felicia react tomorrow to the secret the old woman had kept to herself all these years? A secret made with a promise.

She looked out the kitchen window towards the woods at the rear of the house. Was she watching? The woman who had given up her child so many years ago? The woman who lived alone in a small woodcutter's shack deep in the trees. Was she also thinking of the fulfillment of that long ago promise? The woman shrugged her shoulders and, the dishes done, dried her hands on the worn yellow apron she wore.

She made her way to her room at the rear of the house. She had walled the screen porch in and given the only bedroom in the house to the infant she had raised. A sacrifice she made willingly. She walked over to the dresser on which sat the usual assortment of powders and feminine necessities and opened a small jewelry box. In doing so, she caught her reflection in the mirror. She saw little resemblance of her younger self. Instead, she saw a plump sixty-year old woman with hair that had once been blond and was now faded and yellowed. The blue eyes shining back at her from the wrinkled face were the only features unchanged. They were still bright and shining with God's love. She smiled at the reflection and shook off the melancholy mood that was threatening to overwhelm her. Tomorrow was in the Lord's hands. She removed a small key from the jewelry box and closed the lid.

Slowly, she climbed the small flight of stairs to the second level, wanting to be finished with her search before Felicia returned home. In the short hall, she reached up and, taking hold of a rope above her head, pulled down a wooden ladder that led up into the dark attic. Laboriously, she climbed the ladder, wishing again she were younger when times called for her to make this climb. Reaching the top, she stopped to catch her breath and pulled the chain hanging above her head to turn on a small bare light bulb. The light cut dimly through the dusty darkness and she walked towards the far end of the attic where a chest lay buried beneath old books and worn winter coats. Dust flew, making her sneeze as she unburied the chest and opened the lid. One by one she lifted out mementos of Felicia's childhood. A pink ruffled baby dress the size of a doll's gown, an old porcelain doll with sparse hair and a chipped nose, old report cards, a wrinkled taffeta prom dress and Felicia's first pair of shoes. She set these carefully aside and brought out an old cigar box decorated with brightly painted macaroni noodles. Inside was a letter that had waited for Felicia to read on her twenty-first birthday. A letter that would answer the many questions that Felicia had asked while growing up. It would answer the old questions and bring up a lot of new ones. The old woman glanced at her watch, noted how quickly the time had flown by and keeping out the cigar box, hurriedly replaced the precious items of a bygone time.

"Honey! Where are you?"

"Be right down, Felicia." Taking the box with her, Honey made the slow climb back down the ladder.

Felicia met her at the bottom, hands on her hips. "What are you doing up there?" she demanded. "That's too difficult of a climb for you. I would've gone up and gotten down anything you needed." Felicia noticed the box in Honey's hand and smiled. "What are you doing with that old thing?"

"Never you mind," the older woman told her, putting the ladder back up out of the way. "It's for tomorrow," she added, walking past Felicia and into her room.

"Okay," Felicia said. "I'll humor you. Guess what I did today?"

"I'm too old for guessing games."

"No, you're not." Felicia followed her into the room and flopped belly first across the bed. She ran her hand lovingly over the faded, old quilt that Honey had made. "Come on. I'm humoring you, now you can humor me."

"Oh, all right." Honey sat on the bed beside her. "You went into town."

"Well, that's obvious. You've got to do better than that. Where did I go when I was in town?"

Honey smiled. "Judging by the envelope sticking out of your back pocket, my guess is the post office."

Felicia laughed and reached behind her to retrieve the envelope. "You cheated. Here, read it."

Honey took the envelope and withdrew the letter inside. As she read it, her smile widened. Felicia interrupted excitedly, talking fast. "I got accepted for the position at the children's home I applied for. I'll only be an assistant to start, but they'll help me with college expenses and someday, if I want, I can have a teaching position there or go on into social services. What do you think about that?" She noticed the smile fade on the dear old woman's face. "Why, Honey! What's wrong? Aren't you happy for me?"

Honey rose from the bed and walked over to the window. She parted the lace sheer curtains and sighed. "I just hate to see you leave the safety of this old house. I'll miss my little honey girl." She extended a hand out to Felicia, who grasped it firmly.

"I'll miss you, too. But this is the opportunity I've been praying for. You can't keep me a little girl forever. Besides, I'll be extra careful," she said, kissing the old woman on the cheek. She laughed. "I promise I won't talk to strangers. I won't even look at them." She pulled Honey away from the window. "We've been through this before. I don't understand why you're so afraid. You're the one who taught me I was never alone. That God is always with me. Remember?"

Honey smiled and smoothed the long hair back from the girl's face. "I know He is. It's just an old woman's foolishness. Things will be clearer to you someday. Let's go start dinner. Is Michael coming back later?"

Felicia frowned. "Unfortunately. He's getting to be a real pest. I'm beginning to feel suffocated when he's around." Felicia slipped her arm through the older woman's and they walked together to the kitchen.

"I thought you enjoyed keeping company with him."

Felicia opened the cabinet door above the kitchen counter and removed the dishes they would need for dinner, frowning again when she counted out the third plate. "I used to. Lately he's gotten so serious and very possessive. Saying that it's 'high time' I settled down with him so we could start our own family." She lowered her voice to imitate a man. "Twenty-one is on the downslide as far as marriage goes. How Neanderthal!" She set the dishes on the table and began savagely ripping the lettuce for a salad. "Where does he get his ideas? He's known since high school that I've wanted to teach underprivileged children. This job could be the beginning of my dream."

Honey softly placed her hand over Felicia's. "Don't take it out on the poor lettuce, dear. It's on *your* side. Michael is only echoing the views of ninety-nine percent of the male population in this small town. He'll get used to the idea once your bags are packed and you're on your way."

Felicia placed another kiss on the wrinkled cheek. "You always know just what to say. How did you get so smart?" she teased. Her frown returned as she saw the old blue Chevy driving up the lane leading to their house. "Well, speaking of the devil. The big man is here."

Honey laughed. "Don't call him the devil. Go sit on the porch with him. I can handle dinner. And be nice..." she added as Felicia left the room. "Don't want to spoil anyone's dinner," she muttered under her breath.

"All right," Felicia called back over her shoulder. "We don't want to ruin a growing boy's appetite now, do we?" She slammed the screen door behind her and yelled back an apology. The older woman shook her head and smiled.

Michael stood beside his truck, watching Felicia as she walked quickly towards him. He took in the long, almost black hair clipped up off her neck, the long legs encased in the faded denim jeans and the way her violet eyes sparkled in the fading evening light. *She is beautiful*, he told himself. Felicia's height was the only thing that bothered him as far as her looks went. He was five foot ten inches tall and they stood eye to eye. The only other complaint he had was her stubborn independence. He was determined to straighten her out tonight. She needed someone like him to help her see where her priorities should be.

"Hello, Michael."

He pulled her roughly into his arms. "Hello, doll." Felicia pushed herself away from him and stepped back. "What's wrong now?" he asked, scowling. "We're not playing that stupid game again, are we?"

"It's not a game. I've told you that you're moving too fast. I want you to slow down."

"Slow down! We've been dating since our junior year in high school. I've made myself content with little chaste kisses and hand holding, but gee whiz, girl! We're twenty-one years old for Christ's sake. Act your age! You've got to be the only twenty-one-year-old virgin in the whole state of California!"

"Don't talk like that. You know I don't like it." She turned away. "Like what?"

"You know, plus you're yelling." She began walking toward the porch.

"I am not yelling." He quickened his pace to catch up with her. "Maybe you should yell once in a while. Get the blood flowing. Put some life into that cold, hard shell you call a body."

"Why should I act my age, as you say, if it means giving up the things I believe in? Let's use your own words, Michael. Shall we?" She turned to face him, hands on her hips. "Okay. We've been dating for a long time. You know how I am. Why do you stick around?"

"Because... it's fate. You're my destiny. Besides, I kind of like having the most gorgeous girl in town hanging on my arm. I thought you would get over your Puritan ideas."

"You're serious, aren't you?" Felicia shook her head. "Fate, huh?" She slid her arm through Michael's. "Your parents introduced us. Let's not fight. Dinner's almost ready and we can talk some more afterwards, all right?"

"For a kiss."

"Michael..."

"Just one of your little Puritan kisses."

Felicia laughed and quickly placed a kiss on his lips and jumped back laughing. "Like that?"

"That was the worst yet." Michael laughed with her and reached out to grab her. Felicia sprinted towards the house. Michael quickly caught up with her and they collapsed, laughing, on the front porch swing.

Felicia set the swing in motion with her foot and took a deep breath. "You can't see or hear the ocean from here, but sometimes, when the wind is just right, I can smell it."

Michael placed his arm along the back of the swing behind her. "It's half a mile away."

"I know."

Honey interrupted them with a call to dinner and the two rose to join her. Dinner was relaxed with the three making small conversation. Soon Honey rose to serve dessert.

"So, what's up for tomorrow?" Michael asked as she reentered the room. The question was directed at Felicia, but Michael's gaze met Honey's. The older woman's face paled.

"Not much," Felicia answered reaching out to take the strawberries and whipped cream from Honey. "Why?"

"It's your birthday. Twenty-one. Should be a big celebration. A party or something."

"Oh, Michael. You want to turn everything into a party."

"Hey, Ms. Davis. How about I pick Felicia up tomorrow for a night on the town?" He directed his attention back to Honey. "Show her a little of the nightlife, huh? Maybe...not bring her back. Initiate her in the finer points of life." The words were teasing but Michael's gaze was stony as his eyes met the old woman's.

Honey flinched and looked away. "Let's wait and see what Felicia wants to do, shall we?"

Felicia missed the exchange between the other two as she began passing around the dessert dishes. "Michael, you shouldn't tease Honey like that." She smiled at the other woman. "I think I'd like to spend a quiet evening at home with Honey. How about a rain check?"

Still looking at the old woman, he answered, "Sure. After all, it's *your* birthday."

Honey rose a few minutes later and began clearing off the dishes. "Why don't the two of you go back and sit on the porch for a while? It's a beautiful night. I'll finish up here and head off to bed."

"Are you all right?" Felicia asked, concerned. "You look a little pale."

"Of course, dear. Just feeling my age. You two go on now."

"Come on, Felicia," Michael urged. Felicia nodded and followed him back out to the swing. They settled back into their familiar positions, each reclining against opposite ends of the swing.

"I've got something for you," Michael told her. He started to reach into the pocket of his jeans.

Felicia sat up and turned away. "Let's not, Michael. Not right now."

"Felicia. You're grown now. I'm a man. I have to think of our future. I have needs that need to be fulfilled and I want to marry you." He placed his hands on her shoulders and turned her around to face him. "I saw the cutest little house down the road from my parents. It would be perfect for us."

Felicia pulled away and stood up. "I've told you I want to work with underprivileged children. I'm not ready for marriage."

"You can work with *our* kids."

"Michael. It's not just that. You don't believe in the same things I do. Your dreams aren't my dreams and you have never said one word about loving me. Just that we belong together. Sometimes, I feel like I'm your job or… something. How can you marry someone without love?"

"Dreams!" Michael exploded. "You're basing your life on fairy tales!"

"What about the love, Michael?" Felicia walked to the end of the porch. "What… about… the… love?" She sighed and turned back to him. "I got a letter today. I had applied for a position at a children's home in Sacramento and have been accepted. I start next Monday."

"Without discussing it with me!"

"I told you I was going to apply."

"I didn't think you were serious!" Michael got up and began to pace the porch. Seeing Honey peering at them from behind the front room curtains, Michael jumped off the porch and pulled Felicia with him. Putting his arms on each side of her, he pinned her against the house. "You don't do anything without consulting me," he told her, his face close to hers.

"It's really none of your business," Felicia told him.

"You are my business! You have always been my business!" He slammed a fist into the house. "I have given up my life on you. I grew up being told that I was to watch over you. Keep you in my sights."

"What are you talking about? Michael, you are beginning to scare me." Felicia tried to duck under his arms and Michael pushed her roughly back.

"*You* are my business," he told her slowly.

"That's your problem!" Felicia slapped his hands away. "Michael, I really don't think this relationship is going to work. I hate to end it this way, but I think you need to go. I don't think we need to see each other any more."

Michael struggled to compose himself. "All my life I've been told what a great match we would make. We are perfect for each other, my parents told me. Everyone expects us to marry." He turned roughly away. "What do I tell my parents now?"

"Tell them whatever you want. Tell them that *you* dumped me." Felicia began walking back to the porch.

Michael grabbed her arm. "My parents will have me killed if I let you get away."

"You're exaggerating. Your parents won't kill you. What is wrong with you? Why are you acting this way? Stop it! You're hurting me!" She struggled to release her arm.

"I didn't say *they* would kill me." Michael let go of her arm and took hold of her hand. "I'm sorry. Tonight just hasn't gone the way I planned." He began walking back to his truck. "I'll call you tomorrow."

"I'd rather you didn't."

"I'll call you tomorrow."

Felicia slowly climbed the stairs of the porch and without looking back, entered the house, closing the door quietly behind her. Michael watched her from the seat of his truck. He cursed and slammed his fist against the steering wheel several times until the pain became almost unbearable. Then, slamming his foot to the gas pedal, he sped away, flinging gravel behind him.

Honey looked up from her mending as Felicia entered the room. "I heard raised voices so I thought I would stay up a while to see if you needed me. Is everything all right?"

Felicia nodded. "You know Michael. He can be pretty immature sometimes."

"Oh, I think he knows exactly what he's doing."

Felicia leaned against the wall. "I told him tonight that I didn't want to see him again. He's still talking marriage and gets mad when I say I'm not ready. There's so much I want to do before I settle down and Michael's faith isn't the same as mine. I'm not sure what his faith is." Felicia sighed. "He was talking really strange tonight."

Honey lay her mending in her lap and removing her glasses from her nose, asked, "Do you love him, Felicia?"

She shrugged. "No... I don't think so. At least not the way I imagine I would feel about the man I want to marry someday. He used to be such a good friend." She sighed again and pushed away from the wall. "I'm going to bed. I'm beat. Michael said he'd call again tomorrow so I'll need to be rested up to deal with him, I think." She bent over and kissed Honey's forehead. "Good night, Honey. I do know that I love you."

"Good night dear. I love you, too." Honey watched Felicia disappear up the stairs to her room and allowed a tear to course its way down her weathered cheek. She lifted her heart in prayer for tomorrow as she folded her mending to be put away. She carried the basket of mending with her to the kitchen and peered into the darkness before closing the curtains against the night. Was she watching? The woman from the woods. Was *she* ready for tomorrow?

Chapter 2

Felicia awoke on the morning of her birthday to birds chirping and a gentle breeze caressing her face. She stretched and threw back the blankets before walking to the window to greet the morning. She smiled. She had done the same thing every morning of her life for as long as she could remember.

She loved the way the early morning sun cast shadows through the trees behind the old house and the lawn was sprinkled with the morning dew. Sometimes, if she were lucky, she would spot a deer crossing the yard or a squirrel scampering across the yard. This morning she saw neither. Instead, she was surprised to see a woman standing in the shade of a large oak tree, looking up towards her bedroom window. When Felicia moved the curtain aside to get a better look, the woman quickly darted back into the forest. *Probably someone hiking by and happened across our house by accident,* Felicia thought. Although the woman didn't look dressed for hiking in her summer dress and sandals. They didn't get many surprise visitors down their country road but it did happen occasionally. She shrugged and pulled on a pair of faded denim shorts under the oversized tee shirt she had slept in.

"Good morning, Honey!" she sang cheerfully as she bounced into the kitchen. "You're busy awfully early this morning. Wouldn't be any cause for today to be special would it?"

"You are such a brat," Honey said handing her a plate piled high with pancakes. "Wanted to make you your favorite breakfast for your birthday so sit down and act your age."

"Yummy. You're so sweet. No wonder your name is Honey."

Honey sat down across the table from Felicia. The two bowed their heads while the older woman prayed. "Lord, we ask that you would bless this humble fare and make today a special one for Felicia. Amen."

Felicia echoed, "Amen," and began to eat. She noticed the cigar box sitting in the center of the table and looked up smiling. "So, what's the surprise? I couldn't sleep a wink last night for thinking about it. Are you giving me back the gift I gave you when I was seven?"

Honey pushed the box closer to the girl. "You liar. You've never had trouble sleeping in your life. Here, open it."

Felicia grabbed the box and eagerly lifted the lid. Inside, was a gold locket, slightly tarnished and a sealed envelope with her name on it. She picked up the locket and opened it. Inside was a black and white photograph of a smiling young woman. She looked a few years younger than Felicia was now and was very pretty. Felicia glanced up at Honey and reached for the envelope as the older woman nodded. With trembling hands, Felicia opened the flap and withdrew a single sheet of faded rose-colored paper and began to read silently:

My Dearest Daughter,

Writing this letter is the second hardest thing I have ever had to do. The first was giving you up. I don't regret who I left you with, only that I had to leave you. Alice is a dear and trusted family friend. She is a wonderful Christian lady and I know that she will take great care of you and raise you in God's love. She will undoubtedly raise you better than I can myself.

I requested that she keep this letter from you until your twenty-first birthday. I don't know why I chose that age. Maybe because it's older than I am now and maybe you will have a better handle on life than I do. There are some things that Alice can fill you in on, others I will have to explain when we meet. Oh, Sweetheart, how I long for that day! You are my beautiful baby girl.

Although I left you with Alice, I never really intended to desert you. I can't leave you without promising myself that I will somehow see you grow up. My sweet, sweet baby girl. I fear I may be rambling as I write this letter. How much can I tell you on paper? Only that I love you with all my heart and I so look forward to the day that the dear Lord sends you back into my arms. How empty they feel now. My heart is breaking as I write this. Please remember that I am doing what I honestly feel is best for you.

I love you,

Your mother,

Natalie Elizabeth Wingate

"Wingate," Felicia whispered. "My last name is Wingate." She read the letter a second time. Her senses felt numb. Her pancakes sat growing cold. She had dreamed ever since she was a small child of what her mother looked like and what her name was. She had never felt complete without knowing who she was and where she came from. She looked up to see tears coursing down Honey's cheeks. "Honey?"

"Oh, my dear. How I have dreaded this day!"

Felicia picked up the locket again. "Honey. I saw this woman outside our house this morning. She was standing at the edge of the woods and looking up at my bedroom window."

Honey nodded. "She promised she would somehow watch you grow up. She stays periodically in a shack in the woods."

"The old crazy lady us kids made fun of when we were younger? Why didn't she ever come forward? Why didn't she ever come talk to me?" Felicia began to cry. "I've always wondered who my parents were and my mother was here all this time. Why?"

"I'll tell you what I know. She'll have to tell you the rest." Honey closed her eyes for a second before continuing. "I worked as a housekeeper for the Wingates for several years. They were so proud when Natalie was born. For years they thought they would never have children. She was a beautiful child, but very headstrong. They spoiled her, I'm afraid. She resented the restrictions that her parents put on her because of who they were. They felt they had a certain standard to uphold in the community, I suppose. They were very wealthy. Your roots can be traced back to the Mayflower. Natalie wanted to be like everyone else. She started running with a bad crowd early in high school." Honey took a deep breath. "Before we knew it, Natalie began withering away and withdrawing before our very eyes. She was into drugs and…other things. When she was sixteen, she told her parents that she was pregnant. To prevent a family disgrace they sent her away and sent me with her. We didn't live here at first. We moved around a lot until you were born. Natalie wanted it that way. I moved here with you after your mother left. You were only a few days old. Anyway, your mother told me that she was in danger and you were too, as long as you were with her. She begged me to care for you and to give you my name. She left the locket and the letter for me to give to you on your twenty-first birthday. I moved here to the place where I grew up and raised you as my own. I told people you were the daughter of my younger sister who had died. I never married, so had no children of my own. It was very easy for people to believe that I was your aunt."

"What about my grandparents? Why didn't they want me?"

"They died when their estate burned. It happened a few months after they sent Natalie away. The police determined it was arson and murder. The doors had been boarded shut from the outside." Honey wiped her eyes with the hem of her apron. "They never had a chance to get out. Your mother was left with a very large trust fund. You are actually a very wealthy young woman, Felicia."

Felicia wiped her wet cheeks. "Why was Natalie afraid?" Felicia could not bring herself to yet call this woman her mother.

"She told me that she had gotten involved into something awful and that they intended to take you from her when you were born."

"Who?"

"I don't know, dear. I've told you all I know. Every once in a while I would get some cash sent through the mail with a Sacramento address. Sometimes she would send me a note through my nephew, Dylan. You remember Dylan, don't you? He's actually a second nephew, or something."

"The boy I used to follow around and pester when he spent the summers here? I haven't seen him since I was twelve." Felicia pushed back her chair and stood up. "Does Natalie live in that old shack by the creek that I found when I was small? The one all the kids used to say is haunted?"

Honey nodded.

"Well... I guess I should go meet my...mother."

"Do you want me to go with you?"

Felicia stood silent for a minute. "No... I think this is something I should do myself." The older woman watched sadly as the girl left the room and headed upstairs.

Once in her room, Felicia sat on the edge of her bed and stared into her closet. *What does someone wear for an occasion like this*, she thought as she ran her fingers through her hair. She knew for certain she didn't want to appear in front of her mother dressed in cut off jeans and a tee shirt. She sighed and walked over to the closet and began to rummage through the few dresses hanging there. Piece after piece was discarded on the bed. She wanted to look confident, self-assured. Something she *definitely* wasn't feeling. Finally, she pulled out a white summer dress with spaghetti straps. The dress fell to just past her knees and was embroidered with delicate blue flowers across the bodice. The dress crisscrossed and tied with a thin string in the back. After changing, Felicia walked over to her dresser and picking up her hairbrush, stared into the mirror. The woman who looked back at her looked frightened and unsure. Her pale eyes stood out in deep contrast with her tanned skin and dark hair. Felicia had grown accustomed to people telling her she was beautiful. Would Natalie think so? Felicia thought back to the picture in the locket. The woman pictured there looked petite. Although thin, Felicia's height did not give her the appearance of being frail or petite. She knew now where she got her straight nose and full bottom lip. She sighed and set the brush back on the dresser. She bit her bottom lip, as she often did when she was nervous. Picking up the painted cigar box, she headed out the back door in the direction she had seen Natalie disappear earlier that morning.

As Felicia vanished into the shadows of the trees, Michael stepped out from behind the tree where he had been hiding. He had been eavesdropping through the kitchen window and had heard the conversation between the two women. He had suddenly become aware of why his parents had encouraged him so deeply to court Felicia. He had been assigned as her guard dog. He peeked over the bushes into the kitchen window where he saw Honey cleaning, softly humming a hymn while she worked. He smiled and walked around the corner to the kitchen door and knocked.

Chapter 3

Springtime in coastal California is a beautiful season and normally the walk through the woods would have brought much joy to Felicia. The wind whispered softly through the trees and teased at the hem of her skirt. The sun through the branches dappled the ground and birds serenaded her as she walked. She passed the log where she usually came to pray and spend her quiet time with God. Today, Felicia walked through the beauty without seeing it. Her mind was occupied with meeting the woman who was her mother.

Felicia's anxious heart beat wildly during the half-hour walk to Natalie's cottage and the walk seemed never ending. She stopped just short of the path that led to the front door and took a deep breath, unconsciously straightening her skirt and smoothing her hair. She lifted her eyes heavenward and breathed a short prayer before looking around. The small cabin seemed almost to disappear into the thick foliage and did indeed look uninhabited. Felicia could see that at one time the land around it had been kept clear, but lack of maintenance had let nature reclaim it. The few wildflowers that could survive in the scarce sunlight fought valiantly to capture the dim sunlight. At one time the cabin may have been white but was now faded to a dingy gray with a faded blue trim. The windows were boarded over and a dark fabric could be seen peeking through the holes where the boards had pulled loose.

Felicia was startled to discover that the front door of the cabin had opened and a woman stood there silently watching her. She found herself looking into an older version of the face she had seen in the locket. The woman who stood framed in the doorway had auburn hair cut short and she wore it naturally curling around her face. The blue eyes that may have once shone with innocence were now clouded with worry and lines were beginning to appear around the eyes and mouth. She still had the petite figure of her youth and the prettiness she had once enjoyed when she was young were still very much in evidence.

"Happy birthday," the woman said softly. Her hands were nervously twisting the fabric of the simple dress she wore. She had rehearsed her greeting over and over that morning as she had stood in the shadows of the trees looking up at her daughter's bedroom. She wasn't sure how to welcome this woman who was her daughter. She stepped forward to embrace the girl and thinking better of it, stepped back and offered her hand instead.

Felicia looked down at the hand she was offered and shook it. Natalie motioned for Felicia to join her inside. The small cabin consisted of one room and the inside was in direct contrast to the outward appearance of the cabin. A single bed sat pushed against the far wall with a colorful handmade quilt spread smoothly across it. A crocheted tablecloth graced the small table in the center of the room; two wooden chairs scooted beneath it. A stone fireplace, cold from lack of use, graced one wall and a worn recliner and small end table sat next to it. On the small table was a crocheted doily and a small-framed picture of Felicia as a child. One end of the room served as the kitchen with a few shelves of canned food and dishes and a grill to use instead of a stove. In spite of the plainness of the room, it was clean and homey with its handmade decorations. Nowhere in the room was there evidence of the wealth Natalie had been born into.

"Nice place," Felicia said awkwardly.

"Thank you. It's home." The two women stood silently, watching each other's reactions. Natalie finally pulled back one of the wooden chairs. "Sit down, please." She noticed the cigar box under Felicia's arm. "You got the letter." She gave a small nervous laugh. "Of course you did. You wouldn't be here otherwise. Alice told me that she kept the letter in a little box you made her for Christmas one year. I always wished the present could have been for me."

"How often did the two of you communicate with each other?" Felicia asked, still standing. "It must have been difficult to keep up this lie with constant contact."

"Our communication was sporadic, at best. I know that Alice was aware of my watching you from afar. She caught me once. We rarely speak face to face. I get the impression that she disagreed with my decision to leave you. We mostly corresponded through her nephew the last five years or so."

Felicia nodded. "She told me."

"Please sit down, Felicia." Natalie sat in the chair across the table from her. "I know this is difficult for you. It's difficult for me, too."

"Difficult." Felicia gave a sarcastic laugh. "Yes, I guess you could say it is difficult." She sat down in the offered chair. "I have so many questions, I don't even know where to begin. I feel myself getting angry and I can't seem to get past that."

"I'm sorry. I'll answer your questions the best I can."

Felicia set the box on the table between them. "Here's a good one. How can you possibly answer the question as to why you would give me away and then stand back and watch me grow up? Didn't you want to be my mother?"

Natalie began to cry softly. "Please, Felicia. It wasn't like that at all."

"Then how was it? Oh, that's right. It's here in this letter." She took the letter out of the box. "Honey gave it to me with a 'Happy birthday'."

"I asked Alice to raise you with the notion that your parents had died. Don't blame her."

"She did. Now here I sit, across from a dead woman. You look pretty good." Felicia began to cry. "I spent my life with something missing. A child doesn't always see clearly the fact that their parents had died. They just feel abandoned. Now I know that those feelings were valid."

"You were never alone," Natalie said reaching across the table to take one of Felicia's hands. She drew back, hurt, when Felicia snatched her hand away. She sighed. "I guess I didn't realize just how hard this was going to be." She looked down and folded her hands in her lap. "I was never far away and I knew that Alice would raise you and love you as her own and knowing that the Lord was watching over you every day made it bearable."

"Alice taught me those things and I do believe that the Lord watches over me and that He is better than any earthly father could be. If you also believe that, then why didn't you trust Him to take care of us? You and me. Mother and daughter." Felicia glanced around the room again. "Why is it so dark in here? The shades are all drawn, like you're hiding. Honey told me that you were afraid of someone."

Natalie looked up from her hands. "Let me start from the beginning. Maybe you'll understand things a little better." Natalie bit her bottom lip.

"I do that... Bite my lip when I'm nervous."

Natalie smiled wanly. She prayed silently for guidance. *Oh, God. How do I begin?* She studied the beautiful girl sitting across from her. She didn't see many features of herself. Natalie was only five feet two inches and could see that Felicia was much taller than that. The facial structure was her own but the coloring and height belonged to Felicia's father. As she silently studied her daughter, she could feel the Lord's peace upon her and taking a deep breath, began. "When I was barely sixteen years old I met a man at the party of a friend. He was much older than I was and I thought him the most handsome man I had ever seen. He even looked a little wild and dangerous. Just what was needed to draw me to him. I could hardly believe that he was interested in me. All the things that I found fascinating about Luther, that's your father's name, I knew would make my parents furious and that they would forbid me to see him. I'm sure that was part of my fascination with him. I was becoming quite the little rebel by then. Rebelling against all the restrictions that came with being a Wingate and wealthy and trying not to sully the family name.

"Anyway, I began hanging out at more of the places where I knew he would be. At one of the parties, Luther introduced me to drugs. Drugs that made me feel like somebody else. Somebody important and beautiful. Not long after that, Luther began taking me to "clubs" where everyone wore black robes and nothing underneath. One night I was so high on drugs and believed his words of being someone important, that I didn't resist Luther's advances during one of his special rituals. I became pregnant on top of a sacrificial altar with the group watching. He was telling me that he loved me, although now I know he didn't. During these rituals – there were several – I always woke the next day imagining that I had dreamed it all... until I discovered I was pregnant. I went to Luther before telling my parents. He was deliriously happy. He began laughing and dancing around the room saying all kinds of things that didn't make sense then. How the baby would be a girl and would be a queen. How he would give her to his master to further his position in the kingdom.

"My parents had tried raising me in the Christian faith, or at least their version of it, and I knew that the kingdom Luther was talking about wasn't the one I wanted my baby growing up in. I then went to my parents telling them I was pregnant, but that I didn't know who the father was. They sent me away with their housekeeper, Alice. Before I was sent away, Luther haunted my every move. Everywhere I went I saw him or one of his followers. My girlfriend, the one whose party I had gone to, told me that Luther was going to steal my baby after it was born if I didn't give it to him. She said that I was privileged and would live a life of luxury with Luther. I went to Alice and confided in her and she told me she knew where we could go to hide. The next thing I knew, my parents were dead and our estate burned. I left you with Alice and disappeared, trying to leave traces that I had died in the fire with my parents. I was never sure whether my death was believed or not, so I stayed completely in hiding for ten years. I came out after that to claim my inheritance and went back into hiding again. I didn't let Alice know where I was for several years." During her story, Natalie's eyes had remained fixed on her daughter's face. She watched as Felicia grew more and more pale.

Felicia stared back at her mother as she talked, her eyes growing wider. "You were involved in a satanic cult and I'm the result of *that*?"

Natalie nodded. "I had no idea at the time what I was involved in.

I lived a very sheltered life during my childhood. While I was pregnant with you, Alice shared with me the love of Christ and made clear to me exactly what I had been involved in. I felt so unworthy of Christ's love. It took a lot of convincing on Alice's part and a lot of reading the bible before I could really understand. When I saw the miracle of the beautiful girl He had brought to me out of something so horrible, I didn't want to take any chances on losing you. I wanted you to be safe. So... I left."

"Am I safe, Natalie? I have just found out that my father is some fanatic. I was conceived during a satanic ritual and you left fearing for your life." Felicia's voice began to rise hysterically. "Am I really safe?"

"I don't know. No one has bothered me while I've lived here. I've got money hidden away and it's pretty easy to stay anonymous if you have enough money. People who do know about me think I'm just that crazy woman who lives in the woods and sells her crafts."

Felicia shook her head disbelievingly. "It's all like some crazy movie. Coming out of hiding to claim your inheritance let them know that you weren't dead. If they haven't found you yet, they will." Felicia began to be afraid of what her mother's coming forth may cause. "How does Dylan figure into all this?"

"I needed someone to act as a go-between. I couldn't risk contacting Alice in person. Dylan is a detective and has been able to help me a lot. He's given me a new identity. I'm now known as Lucy Marsh. Dylan has been a gift from God."

Felicia sat silently, running over in her mind the things she had been told. She wanted so much to believe what her mother had told her. It would prove that her mother hadn't left her because she hadn't loved her, but it was hard. At no time in her life had she been witness to anything remotely close to what Natalie was telling her. She thought these things only happened in books and movies.

"Why would Dylan help? Did you explain all this to him?"

"Alice got us together after she caught me watching you one day. Sometime during his days as a detective, Dylan's younger sister was found murdered. The medical examiner, off the record, said it looked like a satanic sacrifice. Once Alice explained my story to him, Dylan was more than happy to help me." Natalie sat back in her chair, the stress of the meeting showing clearly on her face and in the slump of her shoulders. "Dylan has a personal mission in life... to find the murderers of his sister. Seems to think my story and hers may be related and that if Luther ever finds me, Dylan may be able to solve the crime of his sister's death. Dylan wants me to come out of hiding, but has promised not to force the issue."

Felicia looked around the room again. "I can't believe that you've lived here all these years or that *you're* the wicked old witch in the woods that the kids like to sing about. How did you keep me from discovering you? I've played in these woods for as long as I can remember."

"But you thought this place was vacant, right? Or haunted? I never have a fire burning and I keep the windows boarded up so that people think it's vacant. The old witch story was easy enough to circulate. I probably didn't settle here permanently until your teen years. I moved around a lot and stopped by here only a couple of times a year. I've learned to survive."

Felicia stood up. "This is all a little too much for me to comprehend all at once. I have my future all planned out. I've just been accepted as a teaching assistant at a children's home and am finally able to go to college." She shook her head. "I need to be alone for a while to think through all this."

"I understand."

Felicia stood by the front door, her hand on the knob. "You're not going to disappear again, are you? I've wanted to know my mother for as long as I can remember. I really have. I just have to sort through all this." She turned back to the table. "Most children who've been separated from their parents find them after years of searching and then find their parents are normal people living normal lives..." She shook her head again. "I'll be back tomorrow. Maybe...soon, anyway."

Natalie nodded and watched as Felicia walked out the door, closing it softly behind her. Once the door was closed, Natalie lay her head on the table and let the sobs she had been holding in, wrack her body.

Chapter 4

Felicia hurried home faster than she had walked to the cottage. She needed the peaceful sanctuary of her room and the loving arms of Honey. She stopped and frowned when she saw the kitchen door banging open and close in the afternoon breeze. Honey was usually more careful about leaving the loose screen door unlatched. She always said the banging gave her a headache. Felicia shrugged and thought maybe she had left it open when she left that morning and Honey was too preoccupied to latch it. Felicia closed the door behind her as she went into the kitchen, then stopped suddenly and sniffed. She smelled the smoke first, and then saw the flames beginning to crawl up the kitchen curtains.

"Honey?" she called worriedly. She repeated the name more loudly when she saw the old lady resting with her head on the kitchen table. She hurried over to shake her and gasped when the old woman's head lolled back revealing the gaping wound across her throat and the blood pooling on the table and floor around her. "Honey!" she screamed grabbing the old woman into her arms, unmindful of the flames, which were spreading to the kitchen cabinets. Felicia tried staunching the blood with the hem of her dress and was becoming blinded by the smoke and tears.

"Oh my, God!" Natalie moaned from the doorway. She rushed over to Felicia's side. She tried taking the old woman from her daughter's arms. "They've found us, Felicia. They've found us! She hasn't been dead long. We've got to get out of here!" Natalie picked up the cigar box from where Felicia had dropped it. "Quick! Run upstairs and pack a bag. I always keep a bag packed. It won't take me long to grab it."

Felicia shook her head. "I can't leave her." She began to rock back and forth, wailing with the dead woman in her arms.

Natalie glanced worriedly at the spreading flames. "Felicia. We can't help her now. The fire is spreading. We've got to go... now." She turned Felicia's face towards her own. "She hasn't been dead long, Felicia. They'll be coming back. We've got to go."

"You should never have come here," Felicia told her coldly. "This is all your fault. Why are you here?"

"Come on, Felicia!" Natalie jumped up and, grabbing a pan, turned on the faucet, filled the pan with water and tossed in on the curtains in an attempt to slow down the flames. "Hurry, girl!" Natalie screamed as the fire burned her hand. "I followed you because I didn't want our first meeting to end the way it did." She stopped talking and watched the fire spread to the cabinets. "We really have to go now. We'll go to Dylan's. He'll know what to do." Natalie hurried back to her daughter and forcibly removed Honey from her daughter's arms. "If there's something you want to take with you, get it now. I'm not leaving you here. The fire is spreading and if you don't get up now we'll both die here. Alice will have died in vain."

"We have to call the police."

"The police can't help us! Listen to me!" Natalie began screaming at her. "Whoever left those footprints will be back. I know it." Natalie pointed to the bloody tracks that headed to the front of the house. Felicia allowed her gaze to follow Natalie's finger and nodded. Seeming to notice the spreading flames for the first time and beginning to cough, she slowly rose to her feet. "That's a good girl," Natalie told her. "Let's go."

"Just a minute." Felicia ran towards the stairs. "I'll hurry." She sprinted up the stairs and began throwing things into a large duffel bag she pulled from underneath her bed. She grabbed her bible from the nightstand and with a quick glance around the room started back downstairs.

While Felicia was upstairs, Natalie tried laying Honey out on the floor. She didn't want to leave her in the heap in which she had dumped her after pulling her from Felicia's lap. She glanced over at the table where Honey had been lying and saw that she had tried to write something. A pen and paper lay close by and the fire was quickly engulfing the pad of paper. Natalie tried grabbing for it when a hand grabbed her by the shoulder. She screamed and wheeled around.

"Who the *hell* are you?" Michael demanded. "What are you doing here? Felicia!" He began screaming as he peered through the smoke-filled room.

"I'm here, Michael."

"Good." Natalie grabbed her daughter's hand. "The fire is out of control. We'll go back to the cabin to grab my bag and get out of here." She ran out the door, dragging Felicia with her. Michael ran after them.

"Felicia! Who is this woman? What happened back there?" He continued to fire questions at the two women as they ran.

When they reached the cabin, Natalie turned to him. "You need to leave now. You're only in danger by staying with us," she ordered as she ran inside. She grabbed a suitcase from underneath her bed and ran back outside without a backwards glance. "Let's go, Felicia."

"Who are you? Where are you going?" Michael asked, then added as an afterthought, "I have a truck."

"No."

"What do you mean, no?" Michael grabbed Felicia's hand. "Felicia, who is this woman?"

Natalie grabbed Felicia's other hand and tried to pull away. "I'm her mother."

Michael pulled harder. "Felicia told me her mother was dead."

"Stop it!" Felicia screamed, pulling away from them both. "Stop pulling on me. You're ripping me apart! Honey is dead and all the two of you can worry about is who each other is! Please! If we're going, let's go! Michael, drive us anywhere Natalie wants to go."

"I'll drive you straight to the police station."

Natalie whipped a small pistol from the pocket of her dress. "No police," she said, pointing the gun at Michael.

Michael stared wide-eyed at the gun. "Then I'm definitely going with you. Felicia isn't going anywhere alone with a mad woman."

"No."

"Felicia and I are going to be married and I go where she goes."

"Stop it! You're both crazy!" Felicia screamed at them. "Someone will see the fire soon and report it so if we're going, let's go." She took off back toward the road at a run. She stopped next to the house, which was now almost totally engulfed. "Oh, Honey," she sobbed. "You deserved this least of all."

Natalie came up behind her and put her hand on Felicia's arm. Felicia shrugged it off. "Don't touch me." She hurried to Michael's truck, threw her bag into the bed of the truck and got in, scooting over to the center of the seat. Michael and Natalie hurried in on each side of her. As Michael turned the key in the ignition a shot rang out from the woods and the front window shattered, sending them all ducking down in the seat. Natalie tried to peer over the side of the door but could see no one.

"Let's go!"

Michael started the truck and sped off down the drive. "Where to?"

"Just drive north on the 101," Natalie answered. "I'll tell you when to turn. And drive fast."

"Suit yourself." He looked over at Felicia. "What kind of mess are the two of you mixed up in? I show up to take you out for your birthday only to find you holding a dead woman, the house on fire, this woman pointing a gun at me and someone else shooting at us."

"Leave her alone," Natalie ordered. "She's been through a lot today." She glanced over at Felicia who was sitting woodenly between them. She then glanced over at the speedometer. "Why are you slowing down? Speed up!"

"Nobody is following us."

"How do you know that! Michael's your name, right? You haven't looked in your rear view mirror once. How did you get to Alice's? I didn't hear your truck pull up."

Michael looked over at her angrily. "Are you going to boss me the whole time? Because if you are…"

"They are going to think I did it," Felicia interrupted quietly.

"What?"

"Killed Honey. Set the house on fire. The police are going to think I did it. When they don't find my body, I'll be the likely suspect. My fingerprints will be everywhere." She looked up emotionless at Natalie. "Yours, too. We probably erased any evidence the police might have been able to use to find out who did this."

Natalie remembered the burning pad of paper. "Sweetheart, Michael and my prints are there too," she said trying to reassure her. "I doubt if they can find anything with the fire. Once we're somewhere safe, we'll come up with a story and you'll be off the hook."

"I have a better idea," Michael told them. "Let's go back to my parents. We can stay there and then we'll have an alibi."

"I'm sure you'd like nothing better," Natalie told him." Keep driving. And speed up!"

"I need to phone my parents. They'll be worried."

"Not for a while, they won't. If you're that worried about it, stop the truck and hike back. You can always say we stole the truck." Natalie glanced down at Felicia and saw that her eyes were closed but that her lips were moving. Michael noticed it too.

"Great! She's praying! That'll save us." His mouth twisted sardonically. "I guess God is just going to reach down from his busy life and save us."

Natalie patted Felicia's shoulder. "Great idea." She looked back up at Michael. "Why don't you join us?"

He snorted. "I'm not into that whole God thing. Any help we get will come from ourselves."

Felicia opened her eyes and stared silently at Michael's profile. She watched him for several seconds then closed her eyes again. Natalie put her head closer to Felicia's and together they prayed quietly. Michael reached over and turned on the radio.

Felicia sighed and pulled away from Natalie. "Are we going to Dylan's?"

"Yes," Natalie answered. "He's probably the only one who can help us. I know that we can probably stay there for a while. Hopefully, his being a former police officer will be of some help."

"He's a what?" Michael asked, startled.

Felicia laid her head back against the seat. "He's a detective and a friend of Natalie's."

Michael clenched his jaw and swallowed hard. "I thought we weren't going to get them involved."

"I thought you wanted them involved," Natalie answered, taking note of his startled expression.

"Well, I can handle this. We don't need anyone else. Why don't you trust me? Tell her, Felicia. Tell her she can trust me."

Felicia remained silent. "I don't know you," Natalie told him. "You'll have to earn my trust and *that* is hard to do." Natalie made sure Michael saw her put her gun back in her open purse. Michael's face was set in hard lines as he glanced over at her. His expression did not change when he looked back to the highway ahead of them.

"Pull over there," Felicia said, breaking her silence. She pointed to a small service station.

"We need to keep going," Natalie told her.

"And I need to clean up," Felicia told her looking down at herself. She held her blood-covered hands out in front of her. The once white dress was covered from top to hem with blood that was crusting over. "I can't go anywhere with Honey's blood all over me."

"And I need gas," Michael added, turning the truck into the service station Felicia had spotted. He pulled up to the pumps and Natalie sighed heavily before scooting out. Felicia grabbed her bag from the back of the truck and, trying to ignore the stares of the other customers, headed to the service station restrooms.

"Make it quick," Natalie ordered. "I'll head into the men's room and clean up in there to save time."

Michael began filling the tank and noticed the attendant watching them. "We just delivered a difficult calf birth. Came unexpectedly." The attendant nodded slowly and went in to watch them from the service station window.

Felicia closed the restroom door behind her and after checking the other stalls for occupancy, locked the door. She set her bag on the sink counter and caught her reflection in the mirror. She was worse than she had thought. Her hair hung limply around her pale face and the dress was unrecognizable under the blood and smoke stains. She turned on the faucet and held her hands under the steaming water. As the water turned red with blood, Felicia began to cry. She held her hands there until the heat became unbearable and then stripped out of the dress. Her underwear was soiled also. She tossed the dress into the trash along with her bra and underpants and, using the paper towels, began to clean up. She hadn't thought to grab another bra so pulled on another oversize tee shirt over her head without one. She slipped into the pair of jeans she had thought to bring and adjusted the water to a more comfortable temperature. She washed her hair with the hand soap provided and left it hanging wet down her back. She looked into the mirror again, still crying. Her heart ached with the loss of her beloved Honey. Just yesterday, her future looked bright. Today, it only looked bleak. She covered the bloody clothes with paper towels and other garbage from around the restroom then said goodbye to Honey. She began sobbing again and tried ineffectively to rinse her face. Giving up, she let the tears flow and headed back to the truck where Natalie and Michael were waiting.

Natalie had cleaned up quicker and taken the opportunity to buy some provisions from the neighboring convenience store. She stashed these in back along with their bags but kept her purse with the gun in her hand. She watched with a concerned look on her face as Felicia resumed her seat in the truck.

"Back to the 101," Natalie told Michael quietly. "It'll only take us a few hours to get to Dylan's place." She glanced over at her daughter. "Are you going to make it?" she asked.

Felicia looked stonily at her. "I don't really have a choice, do I?" The rest of the drive was made in silence and about an hour later, Natalie pointed out the turn off to Michael.

Chapter 5

Night had fallen by the time the three drove to the half-mile turnoff to Dylan's house, where they were greeted by two large German Shepherds who growled menacingly by the truck doors. Within seconds the porch light to the log cabin they were parked in front of came on. They could see the outline of a large man in the light spilling from the doorway. He whistled for the dogs and they ran to his side, where they sat quietly. The man stood and watched the truck from his porch.

Natalie motioned for the other two to stay in the truck and slowly opened the door. She fully expected to be charged by the dogs and was surprised as they stayed positioned by their master. She walked slowly to the porch. The others watched as the man enveloped her in a big hug. All Felicia could determine through the dark was that Dylan was big. The light behind him kept his features in the dark, but she was able to make out that he was tall and broad shouldered. Natalie and Dylan looked back toward the truck and several minutes later the two in the truck watched silently as Natalie and her friend walked toward them.

"Let me do the talking," Michael ordered.

"Shut up," Felicia said scooting out of the truck. "I'm done having people tell me what to do. *Especially* you." Michael eyed the dogs that had followed their master outside, warily.

"Dylan. You remember Felicia, don't you?" Natalie introduced. Dylan held out his hand and peered through the darkness, trying to decipher her features. Felicia offered her hand in return, shook his quickly and, withdrawing her hand, let it fall back to her side.

"I don't know," Dylan said teasingly. "I remember a little girl that I used to call shadow because she followed me everywhere I went."

"And this is Michael...somebody." Dylan transferred his attention to the young man at her side and offered his hand.

"Moore. It's Michael Moore." Michael offered his name and ignored the extended hand. He reached into the back of his truck and grabbed the two bags.

Dylan frowned slightly at the intended slight. "Well, you must all be tired. My casa is your casa, as they say." He turned to lead the way into the house. Natalie placed her arm around Felicia's shoulders and they followed Dylan, leaving Michael to bring up the rear. Michael glanced over at the dogs as he approached the door and jumped through quickly as they resumed their growling.

"They don't seem to like you much," Dylan commented, smiling as he shut the door on the dogs.

"Good judge of character," Natalie said under her breath.

"Natalie!" Felicia scolded and Dylan laughed.

"Just toss the bags over in the corner, Michael," Dylan instructed. "There's a pot of coffee in the kitchen that's not too old. Anyone interested?"

Felicia nodded and Natalie spoke up gratefully. "I think we could all use a cup."

Michael tossed the bags onto the sofa and sat down in one of the offered chairs. He motioned for Felicia to sit next to him and she declined, and shook her head. She looked around the room. It was bare of any feminine frills, but the colors were complementary. The room they were now in served as both the living and dining area. She could see the kitchen through the door off to the left, and a hallway led off in the other direction. The sofa was striped in dark colors of forest green, navy and burgundy. A braided rug covered the wood floor in front of the stone fireplace and a dark green chair sat in front of it. The fireplace was large and looked as if it hadn't been cleaned in a while and the windows were streaked. In front of the large bay window that ran the length of the room were a wooden table and four chairs. A few pictures of hunting and fishing scenes were scattered on the walls and a rifle hung on pegs above the fireplace. A pair of hiking boots and discarded socks lay tossed on the floor. On the small table next to the sofa sat a small, framed picture of Honey. Felicia walked over and picked it up. A smiling Honey was standing in front of this cabin with her arm around a young, tousle-haired Dylan and an older smiling girl in her teens.

Felicia replaced the picture and turned as Dylan reentered the room with a pot of coffee in one hand and four mugs balanced in the other. Natalie followed closely behind, laden with sandwiches. Felicia studied Dylan as he set the coffee and mugs on the table. He was a strikingly handsome man standing well over six foot in his bare feet. He wore his blond hair cropped short and his hazel eyes shone from the darkly tanned face. His rugged countenance had the look of a man who spent a lot of time outdoors. He smiled up mischievously at Felicia as he caught her watching him. "Handsome, aren't I?" he teased. He motioned for them to all sit down. Felicia smiled up at him timidly and chose the chair closest to Natalie, causing Michael to scowl as he sat across from Natalie. Dylan poured the coffee and slid the cups to their prospective owners, causing some to splash out.

"He's handsome all right," Natalie agreed. "But he's still a slob."

Dylan laughed and leaned back in his chair. The four of them remained silent for several minutes as they drank their coffee and ate their sandwiches. Dylan looked from Michael to Felicia. He hadn't missed Felicia's rejection of Michael's offer for her to sit next to him, or Michael's reaction to that rejection. He had taken an instant dislike to the younger man. His pouting and arrogant attitude turned him off. His years on the police force had given him the ability to quickly assess a man's character and he knew that Michael was not a person he would like. He switched his scrutiny to the woman sitting across from him. Her dark hair fell forward as she blew on her coffee, hiding most of her face, but he had noticed the light colored eyes earlier. He had also noticed the sadness and pallor beneath her tan. He also thought her very beautiful. It had been several years since they had seen each other. Nine years, in fact. Felicia had been twelve and Dylan just twenty-one and fresh out of college. It was hard for him to picture the lovely woman before him as the skinny girl who used to tag along after him and pester him with endless questions.

"Anyone hungry?" he asked. "I could probably dig something up to go with these sandwiches. Some chips maybe."

"I'll get it," Natalie offered. "You just tell me where."

"Cabinet above the dishwasher. If they're not there, try the fridge. I'm always sticking the weirdest things in there." Dylan let his chair fall back to the floor. "I've only got two bedrooms. You ladies are welcome to one. Michael, you're stuck with the sofa. It's pretty comfortable. I'm going to check on the dogs. Be back in a few minutes." Felicia smiled her thanks and watched as Dylan got up and walked out the front door.

"Forget it, Felicia. You're mine," Michael hissed as Dylan left the room. He reached across the table and roughly grabbed her wrist, pulling her up from her chair. She tried to pull away but he held on and moved over behind her, twisting her arm up behind her back, causing her to cry out in pain.

"I'm tired, Michael." Tears welled up in her eyes as Michael twisted harder. "I don't know what you're talking about."

"He watched you the whole time we were sitting at that table! You watched him back! You've stared at him every minute since he came in from that kitchen." Michael put his mouth close to her ear and whispered. "I won't lose you to some pig cop!"

"You're hurting me!"

Michael released her arm abruptly when he heard Natalie reenter the room. Felicia rubbed her aching arm and avoided Natalie's eyes. She was seeing a side of Michael she had never seen before. She'd known that he could be domineering, but now he was abusive. She tried to excuse his actions off to the stress of the day, but there was a new look on his face that scared her. As if he were another person all together. She declined the chips her mother offered her and chose to sit in the chair by the fire. When Dylan came back in, she turned her head away when she saw him looking at her and asked for directions to the restroom.

Dylan watched as she walked away and switched his attention to

Michael. After Natalie had left with the dirty dishes, he walked over to the young man and with his hands on Michael's shoulders, pushed him down into the chair. "Listen buddy. If I ever see you mistreat Felicia the way I saw you treating her while I was outside, you will be picking yourself up off the floor." He straightened up. "You don't treat any woman that way."

"What were you doing?" Michael retorted. "A little detective work through the window? A peeping Tom act, maybe?"

"Just mind what I say, man."

Michael leaned back in the chair and folded his arms behind his head. "Sure. It's your house. You can play the big bad detective man in your own place."

Dylan walked over to the sofa and grabbed the Mexican blanket off the back of it. He tossed it roughly to Michael. "Sleep tight. I wouldn't wander around too much tonight. The dogs sleep in my room. With the door open." Dylan laughed at Michael's startled expression and opened the door to let the dogs in. They looked over at Michael and followed their master upstairs.

Felicia stood in the shower, face up and let the hot water cascade over her. She felt some of the tension and horror of the day dissipate. Why had she been so cowed by Michael at the table? Where was the spunk she usually showed him when he gave her the macho attitude? Why had Michael hurried to join them as they left, not even stopping to let his parents know? He had never really liked her aunt. Felicia shook her head wearily. Too many questions and she was much too tired. Tomorrow she would try to figure things out. She closed her eyes and bowed her head, sending a prayer heavenward for strength and wisdom for herself and Natalie.

Chapter 6

A middle-aged couple let the police into Felicia's aunt's house. The fire trucks had just left and the smell of water and smoke caused the woman to wrinkle her nose slightly, otherwise no expression marred her tranquil face. Once the officer entered, she stepped back onto the porch and stared out at the ocean. Her husband led the police into the kitchen.

"Has anything been moved?" The officer stopped right inside the kitchen door. Everything left from the fire lay under a blanket of powder from the fire extinguisher and water from the hoses. The kitchen had burned completely, leaving only the shell of the outer walls.

The man shook his head and stepped aside as the officer stepped further into the room. He carefully kept his face averted when another woman entered the kitchen and began taking pictures. She looked up as the screen door swung open. The man stepped over and latched it closed. "She must have left it open," he explained. The photographer nodded to Mr. Moore and continued her job.

"Not much reason to latch it now. Mr. Moore," the police officer asked. "Did you know this woman well, an Alice Duncan?"

Mr. Moore shook his head. "My wife knew her slightly from church. The ladies take turns looking in on the elderly and today was my wife's turn. She called the fire department as soon as she arrived and saw the fire."

"She didn't have any family?"

"A niece. My son dated her. I believe she accepted a job in another town." Mr. Moore withdrew a handkerchief from his pocket and wiped his forehead. "I believe she left town a few days ago," he lied.

"Where's your son now?"

"We sent him to town on errands."

The officer stepped over to the back door. "Do you know where this path leads to?" The officer opened the door and stepped outside. Mr. Moore glanced over to where his wife had come into the kitchen. She raised an eyebrow in question. Her husband shrugged and followed the officer outside. They set off into the woods and followed the path to Natalie's cottage. The officer knocked and upon hearing no answer tried the door handle. The door swung open effortlessly. The officer removed his gun from his holster and peered cautiously into the room. "Someone has been living here."

"It's probably a summer cottage," Mr. Moore told him.

The officer shook his head. "No. It's past the season for summer residents." He peered more closely around the room. "Sure you don't know who lives here? Maybe heard something at your church?"

"We've heard rumors from kids about an old witch who lived in the woods," Mr. Moore told him, smiling. "We just passed it off as childish nonsense."

The officer lifted the photograph of Felicia off the table. "Know who this girl is?"

"That's the girl my son is dating."

The officer replaced the photograph and resumed his surveillance of the room. While his attention was diverted, Mr. Moore grabbed the lamp from beside the bed and smashed it over the officer's head. The officer fell to the floor without uttering a sound. Mr. Moore then shrank back as another man entered the room. This man was well over six feet tall and extremely thin. He clothed himself totally in black and kept his head clean shaven. He walked up to Mr. Moore and smiled. The smile did not reach his cold eyes. "Well done," he said, placing a hand on Mr. Moore's shoulder. He walked and stood over the fallen officer's body. "Kill him and dispose of the body. We have already taken care of the photographer. It'll buy us some time." Luther picked up the photograph of Felicia and put it in the pocket of the shirt he wore. He smiled again and took Mr. Moore's hand in his.

"Cover your tracks well. We wouldn't want the authorities to be able to trace anything back to you, now would we?" Mr. Moore slumped in relief as Luther left the cottage.

Mrs. Moore appeared noiselessly beside her husband. "We'd best be on with it," she told him. Her husband nodded and the two of them dragged the unconscious man outside. Mr. Moore took the officer's gun and pointed it to the man's head. He let his hand fall. He was still unnerved from his encounter with Luther.

"Give me that!" his wife demanded. "What if he's still watching?" She grabbed the gun from her husband's hand and without hesitating, pulled the trigger. Together, they dragged the dead man over to a nearby well and watched expressionlessly as they rolled the body into it. The man used his handkerchief to wipe his forehead again while his wife wiped her hands down the sides of her dress.

The woman sighed. "Well, that's that." She looked up at her husband. "Let's get home. I've got dinner in the oven."

Luther didn't usually check personally on the orders he gave, but his frustration over his daughter disappearing led him to feel the need to oversee the murder of the old woman and the covering up of his people's tracks…personally. Although he hadn't committed the murders with his own hands, the satisfaction over their deaths pleasured him immensely. His job required a lot of sacrifice and he intended to reward the ones who followed through with what he asked of them.

Luther slid silently into the back seat of the black Mercedes he had waiting for him further down the road and motioned for the driver to go on. "We are finished here." Luther's voice was low, hypnotic in its softness. Another trait of his never losing control was his ability to seldom raise his voice. He couldn't remember the last time he had had to shout. The driver nodded and started the engine.

Luther leaned back against the leather seat. His anger at seeing his daughter escape with the traitorous witch who had herself escaped him years ago had caused Luther to order the sacrifice of one of his young female followers. Only his master's displeasure could have allowed this woman to escape once again, this time with his daughter.

Chapter 7

Felicia awoke with a start the next morning. She jolted upright in bed, not sure at first where she was. Then the happenings of the previous day passed through her mind, reminding her. She looked over to where her mother had slept and saw that she was already up and gone. She glanced down at her watch. Seven a.m. wasn't too late. She sat up in the bed and stretched, letting her legs hang off the side. The bedroom window had been left open during the night and Felicia got up and walked over to it. The tree outside was full of serenading birds and if she closed her eyes she could almost imagine she was back home in her own bedroom. She reached over and grabbed the denim shorts she had changed into the afternoon before and pulled them on under the Tee shirt she had slept in. She leaned further out the window and heard the heavy thunk of an ax.

Dylan was across the yard chopping wood. She noticed how his muscles bunched under the thin shirt he wore and she tried to compare the strong, virile man she saw with the teenager who used to torment her when she was a child. She shook her head. That was a long time ago. They didn't know each other anymore. Dylan glanced up and saw her watching. He waved and yelled, "Good morning!" before grabbing an armload of wood and heading back to the house. Felicia waved in return and turned away from the window.

"You're up," Natalie announced, walking into the room. "I was just coming to get you. Breakfast is ready. It's so much fun to cook for more than one person." Felicia watched as Natalie fluttered around the room, straightening and talking nervously.

"You should have wakened me sooner."

"You needed your rest. How are you this morning?"

Felicia shrugged. "Better, I think. Yesterday was a lot to handle. You know, you don't have to do that."

"Do what?" Natalie asked, continuing her nervous flitting around the room.

"Talk." Felicia folded her arms across her chest. "Constantly. I mean you don't have to talk just to make conversation, or to distract me."

Natalie stopped her fussing and turned toward her daughter. "I wasn't."

"Yes, you were. I make you nervous."

Natalie smiled. "Yes… I guess you do."

"Well, I shouldn't. I'll be fine, really. How long are we going to stay here?" she asked, changing the subject. "I realize that it's probably not feasible to go home. Especially with being shot at. But we can't stay with Dylan indefinitely. I think Michael is going to cause problems here and we need to call the police. They're going to want to know why we didn't contact them right away."

"Let's give things a few days. Take some time to think things through." She put her arm around Felicia's shoulder. "We're together now. God is in his heaven. The sun is shining. All is right with the world."

Felicia smiled sadly. "Honey use to say that to me when I would get upset. I don't think now is an appropriate time. All is not right."

"She's the one who taught it to me. I'm sorry to make light of what you're going through. Let's go eat. Prince Charming is beginning to stir and is complaining about being hungry."

The two women walked into the dining room together and frowned. Michael was already seated and had begun to eat. "You could have waited for the rest of us," Felicia told him.

"Why? I was hungry."

"Obviously."

"Felicia, go get Dylan, will you?" Natalie asked. "I'll fill the rest of the plates and bring them out, since Michael couldn't seem to bring himself to do it." She looked sternly at the young man who ignored her and continued to eat.

Felicia walked outside and stopped just outside the door, leaving her hand on the doorknob as the two German Shepherds loped around the corner of the house. They walked to the bottom step and sat down, watching her. She tried to smile calmly and slowly stepped forward. When she reached the bottom step she had to stop. The dogs weren't moving. They just sat there silently, their eyes never leaving her. "Dylan?" she called. "Would you please call your dogs?" A shrill whistle pierced the air and the dogs bounded off the way they had come. Felicia followed them.

Dylan had just finished stacking the wood and had his head stuck in a barrel full of rainwater. He slung back his head and smoothed the water from his hair. He looked up as Felicia laughed. "What?" he asked, looking confused.

"You used to shove my head under the water when I would annoy you too much. Don't you wash up in the house?"

He grinned. "This is easier. Plus, the water feels good. Are you in the mood for a dunking?"

"No thanks! Natalie sent me out to tell you that breakfast is ready."

Dylan grabbed the shirt he had laid across the stack of wood and slung it over his shoulder. "Why don't you call her mom?"

"I just found out yesterday that I even have a mother. I'm having a little trouble coming to grips with everything. You know…with Honey dying and Natalie turning up so suddenly." Felicia stopped abruptly and looked up at Dylan.

Dylan smiled sadly. "I know about my aunt. Natalie told me last night. So… she told you all about her past, huh? Try giving her a break. She's gone through a lot and only did what she thought was best."

"Yeah, well." Felicia answered back sharply. "Her best didn't make things go away, except me, did it? We're in the same boat now that she tried running away from when I was born!"

"I'm sorry." Dylan took her arm. "Leaving you was the hardest thing she ever did."

"You ought to know," she retorted, yanking back her arm. She turned back to the house. "You saw her more than I did."

He nodded and slung his arm around her shoulders, noticing how she winced and glanced up at the house, but didn't pull away. He frowned a moment, pushing back the urge to storm up to the house and punch Michael in the mouth. "Let's eat."

Michael was leaning back in his chair, finished eating by the time the other three sat down. He noticed Dylan remove his arm from around Felicia so he could open the door. Felicia looked his way and returned his stare. She chose the chair farthest away from the young man and started to eat.

When they were finished and Natalie was refilling everyone's coffee, Dylan asked, "Natalie told me last night that the three of you needed a place to stay for a while. I didn't ask any questions then, but I am now. What exactly happened to my aunt? Natalie told me a little last night, but I think there's more to the story. Why are the three of you hiding?" Natalie and Felicia glanced at each other and both bit their bottom lips. Dylan noticed the action. "You two do some of the same things, you know that?"

Natalie sighed. "Yesterday, Felicia came to see me and when we returned to your aunt's house she was dead. I told you that part. I didn't mention that she had been murdered."

Dylan raised his eyebrows and looked around the table. "Murdered? How?"

Felicia stood up, tears welling up in her eyes and continued. "She gave me Natalie's letter for my birthday and I went to Natalie's house. When I got back she was dead. Her throat had been cut and the kitchen was on fire." Felicia began to cry.

Dylan threw his coffee mug across the room with a curse. The other three jumped as it shattered against the wall, sending the dark liquid streaking down the wall. "Not again," he muttered, hanging his head.

Natalie jumped up and ran over to him. "What again, Dylan? Tell me. Do you know something about yesterday?"

"You remember I had a sister, right? Her name was Susan." Natalie nodded and leaning forward, propping his elbows on the table,

Dylan continued. "She was killed and the closer I got to finding out about her killers, the more people that were found dead. Usually with their throats cut."

"Doesn't mean it's the same thing, or the same people," Michael uttered.

"So you know who killed Honey?" Felicia asked.

"I'm just speculating. After Susan was killed, I discovered, during my investigation, that she had been involved with a cult. The same one that Natalie had run away from many years ago. The chances of Natalie reentering the picture – and my aunt suddenly being killed – leads me to believe that they knew, or suspected, where Natalie was all along."

"So, mister hot shot detective," Michael asked sarcastically. "Where are these people?"

"Northern California, somewhere. A cult calling themselves "Children of Light". We know that Luther hangs out in Northern California. It's rare to see him, but he has been seen a few times around Sacramento. Deaths are spread around and suspects are never located. Things happen sometimes around the Oregon border and sometimes in Washington that all seem to point to his followers."

"How do you know it's him?" Felicia asked. "It could be another cult or not a cult at all."

"It's the same one, all right," Dylan answered as Natalie began clearing off the table. "Luther likes to leave his calling card. Either burns or cuts a big L in his victim's chest or on the ground somewhere in the direct vicinity. All his followers have an L tattooed on their right shoulder. Show her, Natalie."

Felicia glanced up at her mother in alarm. Natalie pulled down the neck of her blouse to show a smooth scar where a tattoo had been removed. "I had it removed after you were born."

"Was there an L anywhere around my aunt's body?"

Natalie shook her head. "No. But we could have surprised them. It did look like she tried to write out a couple of letters. There was a pad of paper near her, but it was on fire by the time we got there." She glanced up as Michael made a choking sound. "I couldn't make them out clearly though. Maybe an M. But it could have been an L, I suppose."

Michael grinned sardonically and turned his attention back to Dylan. "What now? You're the expert here. Surely you have a plan to get us out of here."

"Yeah. I'm going for a walk." Dylan stood up. "Make yourselves comfortable. I'll be back in a while."

"Care if I join you or would you rather be alone?" Felicia asked quietly.

Dylan looked over in surprise. "No, come on ahead."

"I need to call my folks," Michael spoke up. "I'll be heading into town."

"I have a phone here."

"I'd rather go into town."

"I'd rather you didn't."

Michael stood up angrily. "Look mister. You have no right to dictate to me what I can, or can't do. I have a truck and I can ride into town whenever I want."

"Big man. Have truck." Natalie added from where she had sat back down. Natalie and Dylan laughed while Felicia stood off to the side, nervously watching the exchange between the two men.

"I said... I don't think that it's a good idea," Dylan repeated. "We need to keep a low profile."

"We? We?" Michael almost shrieked. "Since when did you become a part of *our* we?"

Natalie spoke up giggling. "Michael, stop while you're ahead. You're sounding more ridiculous with every word that comes out of your mouth." She stood up from the table. "We came to Dylan for help. He didn't ask for us to dump all this on him. I think we should listen to him and I also think he's right about you staying here."

"Well...you just watch me!" Michael strode angrily toward the front door and flung it open. Dylan's dogs met him at the porch and silently sat guard at the foot of the steps. Eyeing them carefully, Michael walked slowly past them. Dylan reached up above the fireplace and withdrew his shotgun. As Michael reached the truck,

Dylan took careful aim and blew out the front right tire. Michael yelped and jumped back. He cursed and yanked the driver's door open and turned the engine. "I have a spare," Michael yelled out the window. Dylan shot out the other front tire. Michael cursed again and struggled to turn the truck around on its rims. By now Dylan had come outside and down the steps. He carefully and methodically shot out the other two tires.

"How about four spares?" he asked, grinning.

Felicia watched in shock as Dylan marched back in the house and calmly replaced his gun above the fireplace. He turned around and winked as Natalie collapsed on the sofa in laughter. Felicia glanced back out the door and smiled as she watched Michael marching around his truck, cursing and kicking at the tires.

"Care for that walk now?" Dylan asked, offering her his arm. She nodded and looped her arm through his. They watched in vain as Michael jumped in his truck and drove off on his tire rims.

"He is a very stubborn man," Felicia pointed out.

"He's obnoxious. I don't trust him. Something about him bothers me. Just why is he so anxious to go into town?"

"Natalie doesn't trust him either. Hasn't from the moment they met each other in Honey's kitchen."

"He was there?"

She nodded. "He was there when we came back from Natalie's. He says he found Honey's body first and then came looking for me."

Dylan remained silent for a moment, thinking. "There's a little creek that flows about fifty yards behind the cabin. Has a great log just perfect for sitting." He led the way south, away from the cabin. "That's where I go when I want to be alone and think things through. *This* definitely needs thinking through." They could hear the dogs barking up ahead.

Felicia laughed. "How much more alone do you want to be living way out here?" She looked around them, taking in the beauty and solitude of the place. "It's beautiful out here, Dylan. How did you find this place?"

"My father left it to me." They had reached the log and stream that Dylan had mentioned and sat down. "Felicia?" he began as he sat down. "How long have you known Michael?"

"As long as I can remember, why? We grew up together."

"Has he always treated you so roughly?"

"No. He's always been bossy, but usually I'm okay going along with whatever he wants. It wasn't until recently, when I decided to move away, that he got really insistent, why?"

"Just a feeling. It bothers me that he wanted so strongly to use a phone in town rather than mine here, knowing the danger that the three of you are in. I just don't get it." He thought for a minute. "Have you ever seen him with his shirt off?"

"No! What are you implying?"

"Not that! Something is nagging at me."

"I don't think he's dangerous. He would never hurt me." Felicia bent over and trailed her fingers in the cool water of the stream. She looked around at the thick foliage around them. It was so cool and peaceful there under the trees.

Dylan shrugged. "Maybe, but I've heard cases of Luther assigning one of his people as guards over people that he as a special purpose for. I'd say that you being his daughter might mean he has a special purpose for you."

She shook her head. "I think you're really stretching things now."

Dylan shrugged again. "What are those dogs barking at?" He stood up. "Stay down. This isn't like them." He pulled a revolver from the back of his jeans and looked around.

Felicia sighed. "Does everyone carry a gun around here? Natalie has one in her purse."

Dylan whispered back. "Can you shoot?" She shook her head. Dylan grabbed her hand and led her off in the direction of the dog's barking. A short way down the stream they found the remains of a campfire and pine branches piled up off to the side. Dylan ordered the dogs to be quiet and peered up into the tree where they had been barking. He motioned for Felicia to stay behind him.

"What is it?"

"Come down out of there!" Dylan ordered.

"Dylan?"

"No way!" a voice called down. "Your dogs will eat us."

"Look, son. I'm a police officer." Dylan showed him his gun. "And I'm ordering you to come down out of that tree! If you don't, I'll send the dogs up the tree after you!"

"Dogs don't climb trees!"

"These are special tree climbing dogs." Dylan winked at a confused Felicia. "Want to see?"

They watched as a young boy dressed in dirty blue jeans and a tattered T-shirt climbed down.

"It's a little boy," Felicia said, surprised.

"I'm not little. I'm ten." The boy stood proudly before them. His brown hair was tousled and long, hanging over the neck of his shirt, and there were dark smudges under his brown eyes.

"What are you doing up my tree, son?" Dylan wanted to know.

"Getting away from your dogs. What do you think I was doing up there? Sight-seeing?" the boy smarted back.

"Before that."

"Camping."

"In my woods?"

"I don't see your name anywhere."

"What's your name?" Felicia bent over to be on the boy's level.

The boy eyed her suspiciously. "Mark. My name is Mark."

"My name is Felicia," she told him. "And this rude man, is Dylan. Are you here alone?"

"Yes."

"No." another voice answered from up in the tree.

"Lisa! I told you to be quiet!"

"But I want to get down, Mark. My bottom is getting sore from this branch."

Dylan peered back up into the tree. "Come on down, honey."

"I can't."

"Why not?"

"I'm too scared to come down!"

Dylan sighed and shook his head. Tucking his gun back into the waistband of his jeans, he proceeded to climb the tree. Nestled in the branches, too high for him to climb, sat a smile, blonde girl, her eyes wide with fright. "You'll have to climb a little," he told her. "Those branches aren't strong enough for me." She shook her head, then nodded and began to slowly inch her way down to him. When Dylan could reach her, he took her under the arms and slung her onto his back. "What's your name, honey?"

"Lisa," she answered.

"Okay, Lisa. You hold on real tight and I'll get you down." She nodded and tightened her grip around his neck. Dylan began to back slowly down the tree. When he reached the bottom, Felicia took the girl from him.

"Where are your parents?" she wanted to know. "It's too dangerous for the two of you to be out here alone."

"They're gone!" Lisa wailed.

Mark shushed her and explained. "They went to the store about a month ago and never came back. We're looking for them."

"Why didn't you call the police?" Dylan asked.

"They won't help us. They'll only put us in an orphanage or something."

Dylan sighed again. "Maybe…for a little while. But they probably could have found out what happened to your parents. Do you live around here?"

"Not far. Well, we did."

"What kind of work do your parents do?"

Mark shrugged. "I think he was a salesman or something. He was always going to meetings and people were always coming over and staying the night in our basement. It was part of his business, he said."

"Sometimes they wore funny robes," Lisa piped up.

Felicia and Dylan glanced at each other, startled.

"How have you been taking care of yourselves?"

"I took care of us," Mark said proudly. "We're doing just fine by ourselves."

"We ate food out of garbage cans!" Lisa exclaimed. "It was

gross!"

Felicia pulled the little girl close. "Garbage cans! Dylan we have to get these two back to the house and get them something to eat."

He nodded and motioned for them to stay still a moment. "There's something that doesn't make sense here. Mark, you said your dad was a salesman and now he's gone." The boy nodded. "And Lisa, you said that people came over in funny robes..."

"She shouldn't have said that!" Mark interrupted.

"Why not?" Dylan asked.

"Dad said it was private business!"

"Have your parents ever left the two of you alone before?"

"Never." Lisa answered. "But daddy said he wanted to..."

"Lisa!" Mark shouted.

"I think you should tell us, Lisa." Dylan told her. "We're trying to help you."

Lisa nodded. "Daddy said he wanted to quit his job and that his boss was mad. One night I overheard Mommy crying because Daddy's boss wanted me and Mark to come and live with him."

"Aw, man!" Mark moaned. "We're in trouble now."

"No you're not," Felicia assured him. "We're going up to the house right now to get you something to eat and a nice warm bath." She looked over at Dylan "No more questions right now. These children are tired."

Natalie had stood at the window and watched as Felicia and Dylan disappeared into the woods. With Michael gone also, the quietness consumed her. She fetched her bible from the bedroom and curled up in the dark green, easy chair. She didn't open the book. Instead, she clasped it to her breast and let the sobs she had been keeping in over the last day wrack her body. As she cried, her soul strained toward heaven, seeking refreshment and encouragement. She felt the twenty-year-old fears threaten to consume her. She had wanted her daughter's birthday and their reunion to be special. Not overcast with disaster. She didn't know how long she sat there, but the next sound that came to her ears was the voices of Felicia and Dylan as they came around the corner of the house. She heard other voices joining theirs and, wiping her tears with the back of her hand, turned to greet them as they came through the door.

"Natalie? Are you all right?" Felicia asked, noticing her red eyes.

"I'm fine, dear. Just visiting old ghosts for a minute." She noticed the two children hanging back by the door. "Who are our guests?" She turned a questioning look toward Dylan.

"We found them out in the woods. Seems they've been living on their own for a while. They seem to have been camping here. Not very long, though. I think Luke and Duke would have found them sooner, if it were longer than that." Dylan reached into the refrigerator and tossed bread and sandwich meat on the counter. "Said their parents just up and left them about a month ago. Sounds fishy to me. Lisa spoke about secret meetings being held in their basement." He handed Natalie some juice. "I think these two could possibly be mixed up in what's going on with you. Maybe not directly, but definitely something similar."

Natalie sighed. "The last thing we need is the added responsibility of two little kids."

"I agree. I'll try taking them into town on Monday. Is Michael back? I don't like him being gone this long."

"No. I hope he doesn't come back. I detest that young man. Always have. Ever since I saw him as a teenager following around after Felicia."

The two began making the sandwiches. "Are they getting married?"

"I don't think so. Maybe on his part." She put the finished sandwiches on a tray. "I think Felicia has been trying to slowly distance herself from him." She walked into the dining room. Two clean children, dressed in adult size T-shirts sat waiting patiently at the table.

"Hey, man!" Mark yelled. "You didn't tell me you had horses!"

"You didn't ask."

"You didn't tell me either," Felicia scolded playfully.

"Yeah, I have a couple. Would it have made you a little more excited about coming home with me if you had known?"

"You bet!" Mark took a big bite of his sandwich and mumbled through a mouthful. "I ride good, but Lisa doesn't. She's scared."

"Am not!" Lisa grabbed her sandwich. Natalie and Felicia smiled at each other over the children's heads.

Dylan sat down across from the two children and leaned his elbows on the table. "Okay, guys. Spill your guts. What kind of business was your father in?"

Mark shrugged. "Never was too sure about that. Didn't make much money though. We didn't even have a Nintendo. Can you believe that?"

"I think Dad got fired the night he left," Lisa added.

"Why's that?"

"Well... This man came over one day and they were fighting. They were really yelling at each other. Daddy said he wanted to quit and the man said nobody quit. Mommy began to cry and that was when I heard them talking about Mark and me. Then the man just left."

Dylan frowned. "What did the man look like?"

Lisa shrugged, and Mark answered. "He wore black. They all wore black. And his hair was real short, like my Dad's. Like an army man's hair is. "

"Did your dad have a tattoo on...?"

"Peace is over," Natalie interrupted. Michael drove up the driveway on four new tires.

"Hey! Who are the rug rats?" he asked, plopping down into a chair. He reached over to grab a can of soda and Natalie moved it away from him and handed it to Mark.

"This food is for the children. If you're hungry get up and fix your own. After running off the way you did, you're on your own."

"I don't like him," Lisa whispered to Mark. He hushed her and pulled her chair closer to his.

Michael stood up angrily. "I ought to take Felicia and leave right now. I never wanted to come here in the first place."

"I see you got new tires," Dylan said.

Michael switched his attention to Dylan. "I had to get new rims too, thanks to you!"

"You're welcome. I didn't tell you to take off with no tires. You must have pulled over into Wheeler's Station. There's no way you could have made it into town otherwise."

"Yeah… I did. I called my parents from there. They were worried sick. Seems they drove over to your aunt's and found the body. Then they called the police and the fire department. Mom about fainted. Thought maybe Felicia and I had been kidnapped or something."

"What did you tell them?" Natalie asked worried.

"Relax. I just told them that we decided to take off for a couple of days. Said Felicia's aunt was alive when we left." He winked at Felicia. "Told them we wanted privacy while we planned our wedding. I acted real surprised about the old lady's death."

"That, *old lady,* happens to have been Honey!" Felicia told him, raising her voice.

"How easy the lies just roll off your tongue," Natalie told him. "Come on, kids. Let's go find those horses Dylan says he has. I think there might even be some carrots in the fridge." They jumped up, sandwiches in hand, and followed her through the kitchen.

"Felicia," Dylan said. "Let's you and I go finish what I had originally planned on doing today."

"What's that?" Michael demanded, grabbing Felicia's arm.

She jerked herself free. "Dylan is going to teach me to shoot." She hurried past him and out to the porch.

"I could teach you," Michael whined as he followed them outside. "I didn't know you wanted to learn. I'm a really good shot."

"That's okay, buddy," Dylan patronized. "You can just watch and relax. You might learn something."

Dylan took some soda cans from a burlap bag hanging on the porch and set them up along the fence, facing the woods. He pulled the gun from the waistband of his jeans and began to show Felicia how to hold and load it.

"Hey! What kind of gun is that?" Michael yelled from his viewpoint on the porch.

"It's a .44 magnum. Want to see it?" Dylan asked, pointing it in his direction.

Michael jumped up. "Don't point it at me! It might go off!"

"Might," Dylan laughed and turned back to Felicia.

"You shouldn't play around with him like that," she whispered.

"I know. I couldn't resist. That guy gets under my skin." Dylan stood behind Felicia with his arms around her, placed his hands over hers and leveled the gun.

"Good grief!" Michael yelled again. "Do you have to maul her?"

"Ignore him," Felicia said, trying to concentrate. Dylan's closeness made her nervous, yet she felt safe in his arms and was enjoying the feeling. Better than she felt around Michael, anyway.

"Now," Dylan instructed. "It's really easy. You just gently pull the trigger."

"Like this?" Felicia jerked and the shot went wild, striking a nearby tree and leaving a wide gash in the bark.

Dylan laughed. "With your aim, whoever you point at should feel pretty safe."

She blushed. "Let me try again. You stand over there." She pointed and Dylan went to stand by the porch where his dogs were lying, keeping their eyes on Michael. Michael glared at Dylan and crossed his arms over his chest. Dylan leaned against the porch railing and copied Michael, folding his own arms across his chest. Felicia glanced over at the two before turning her attention back to the row of aluminum cans. She squinted down the barrel and pulled the trigger. She missed.

"You closed your eyes," Dylan called to her.

"No, I didn't."

"Yes, you did. Look at your target. It's still there." Dylan laughed. "Want to go again?" Felicia clamped her lips tightly together, spread her legs slightly for support, and shot again.

"She's beautiful, isn't she?" Michael moved over to stand close to Dylan, talking softly. "Too bad. She's mine. She belongs to me. You hear?" Michael smirked and went into the house.

Dylan turned to say something back to him and missed Felicia's first can go sailing off the fence. "I did it! Dylan, did you see that?"

She ran up to him, pleasure lighting her face. "Only took me three tries, but I did it. Can I go ahead and keep shooting?" He laughed with her and nodded. He watched in enjoyment as she loaded the gun the way he had shown her, and set three out of four more cans flying off the fence. She was a pleasure to watch. She had left her hair down and the slight breeze that was blowing that afternoon gently blew it around her face. Her eyes sparkled with enjoyment. He took time to admire her long legs in the shorts she wore and when she turned around, he realized he had been staring and walked toward her.

"Yes, she's beautiful," he said to himself.

"What?"

"Nothing. You did great, but let's move on to a self-defense lesson. This is my favorite part." He took the gun and stuck it back into his waistband. "I get to hug you. I'm the bad guy. Pretend I'm Michael."

"Oh, really." She put her hands on her hips.

"Pay attention. I'm going to come up behind you and grab you. Like this." He demonstrated by wrapping his arms around her waist.

Felicia laughed. "And I flip you like this, right?" She grabbed his arm, bent over at the waist and thrusting her hip into his stomach, flipped him easily over her shoulder. She laughed as he lay on the ground looking up at her, astonishment on his face. "I took self-defense in high school."

"You could have warned me. Knocked the breath out of me." He stood up and dusted himself off. "Plus, the ground back here isn't the softest landing. I fell on my gun, too. Probably leave a bruise."

"You deserved it, you flirt," she told him laughing.

"Reminds me of old times," Natalie said, walking up to them. "I used to watch the two of you playing from the edge of the woods."

"The horses are swell!" Mark interrupted, running up to them. "They ate a carrot right out of my hand."

Lisa walked up and slid her hand shyly into Felicia's. Felicia smiled down at her, pleased. "Guess I've made a friend, huh?" Lisa smiled back and leaned wearily against her. Noticing the child's fatigue, Felicia made the motion that beds be prepared for the kids in a corner of the living room. Dylan agreed and set off in search of more blankets.

"Guess I'll see what I can round up for dinner. Dylan is getting low of food," Natalie said. "One of us will have to go into town soon." The little group rejoined Dylan in the living room.

"I'll go tomorrow," Dylan called from the hall. "You three don't need to be seen."

Michael laughed. "You are too much. No one knows where we are, much less looking for us out here in the middle of nowhere."

"Natalie, could you help me in here?" Dylan called from the closet. "We'll leave early. Before Michael wakes up," he whispered when she arrived. "We need to get Felicia a fake ID and I don't want Michael to know about it. You're right. I don't trust him. I plan on ditching him at the first opportunity."

Michael transferred his attention to the two children after Natalie left the room. He stared quietly at them for several minutes, not saying a word. When they finally noticed him watching them, he patted the sofa beside him. Lisa shook her head and scooted closer to Mark.

"He scares me," she whispered.

"Don't worry. I won't let anything happen to you." Mark put his arm around his sister and returned Mark's stare.

"A pretty little girl and a spunky little boy," Michael said. "How sweet. Come on over here, sweetheart. I won't hurt you. I'm Felicia's boyfriend. We're getting married. You like her, don't you?"

"You're lying!" Lisa blurted out. "She wouldn't marry someone like you!"

"What do you know, you little brat!" Michael hurled one of the sofa pillows at her.

"Michael, what's wrong with you? Leave them alone," Felicia told him.

"We were just playing. Weren't we, sweetie? I just got a little rough." He got up and walked over to ruffle the child's hair.

"Don't touch her!" Mark yelled, launching himself at Michael. "Never touch her!"

"Hey! What's all the commotion in here?" Dylan asked, coming back into the room. He and Natalie entered just as Mark attached himself to Michael's back.

"Just a little rough housing," Michael answered, removing Mark from his back. He put his hand on the boy's shoulder and squeezed tightly. "Right, buddy? Just playing?"

Mark winced, and nodded.

"Well, I think it's time for two little children to go to sleep," Natalie told them. "Why don't the two of you sleep in there with me and Felicia, after all?" She glanced up at Dylan. "That way they won't be encouraged to play." Dylan nodded and watched the two women lead the children off.

Chapter 8

Michael was already awake when the others got up the next morning so Dylan had no choice but to take him along. Michael kept up a stony silence all the way into Sacramento, his arm across the back seat, keeping Felicia firmly against his side.

Several minutes into town, Dylan pulled the car over in front of a grocery store and the group got out. Natalie handed each of the adults a list of provisions to buy and they waited until Michael had separated himself to begin on his list.

"All right, everyone else hurry back to the car," Dylan told them. "He'll figure out we're gone soon enough."

Felicia kept glancing back over her shoulder as they walked out of the store. "What are we going to tell him when we get back?"

"We should leave him here," Mark suggested.

"Not yet, pal." Dylan told him, closing the rear door after the kids. "We'll wait until the time is right."

"Promise?" Lisa wanted to know.

Dylan winked at her and slid behind the wheel. He glanced over his shoulder for a break in the traffic, and quickly merged the Bronco onto the freeway. "We'll have to stay tightly together," he told everyone. "The part of town we're going to isn't a very safe one."

Dylan drove for several minutes before pulling off the freeway and driving to the back of a seedy bar in the middle of Sacramento's inner city. It was called Ramon's. They emerged from the Bronco in an alley that ran the length of Ramon's. Felicia looked around and saw overturned trashcans; litter spilling out and profane graffiti was sprayed over every available surface. A vagrant was propped up against the stairwell they were climbing and Felicia could smell the alcohol on him. It was strong enough to make her wonder if he had bathed in it. She wrinkled her nose and followed Dylan to the back door. Lisa jumped and shrieked when a cat dashed out of one of the trashcans, sending it banging against the wall of the building. Ramon's was a large peeling structure that had definitely seen better days.

"Natalie and I already have fake identification. Natalie also has papers giving her a whole new identity. I think just a new ID will be okay for Felicia."

"What do I need it for?" she asked. "I'm not getting a whole new identity?"

"I don't think that's necessary right now. I'm serious about tracking down Luther, but on *my* terms. If we need to show ID, for any reason, hopefully it could throw him off our trail for a little while at least. I want to find him, if possible. Not have him find us. Keep your fingers crossed."

"Praying is more of a sure thing," she told him.

"You pray and I'll keep my fingers crossed." Dylan turned to Natalie and the kids. "Natalie, help keep those two close, and don't let them touch anything." She nodded.

They walked up to a peeling blue door and Dylan knocked, once, twice, then once more. A small window opened high up in the door. "Yeah? What do you want?"

"Ramon."

"He ain't here. Ain't no kids allowed anyway."

The two children stepped closer to Natalie. "We have money," she told him. "Plenty."

"I told ya. Ramon isn't here."

Dylan sighed. "Tell him the Baloney Man is here." The window closed.

"Baloney Man?" Felicia asked.

Dylan smiled. "Yeah. He used to always tell me that I was full of it." Felicia raised an eyebrow. They stood outside for several minutes before the window in the door opened again.

"Ya packin? If you are, slide it through the window, barrel first."

Dylan and Natalie both handed over their guns and the door slid open.

"Hold it." They were stopped by a large, burly man, wider and tall than Dylan, who stood at six foot two. "Turn around, hands on the wall." He searched Dylan first, causing Dylan to grunt in pain a few times. When it became Natalie's turn, she closed her eyes and bit her lower lip while she endured the man's thorough search. Felicia watched in alarm as the man's hands went under Natalie's blouse, checking her bra then up the legs of her shorts. She looked over at Dylan, her fright showing in her eyes. He tried to smile reassuringly. "My, my," the man said as he turned her to face the wall. "You're a pretty one." She flushed red and stared straight at the wall as the humiliating search went on. When he had finished, the man turned her back to face him and softly caressed her cheek. Felicia stared straight ahead and the man chuckled. When he turned to the kids, Dylan stopped him.

"Not the kids, man. They're clean."

"Gotta check everyone. I got my orders."

"Not the kids," Dylan told him firmly. "I'll take it up with Ramon myself." Dylan stood his ground and the man stared silently at him for several seconds, then he shrugged and motioned for them to follow him. He led them into a surprisingly plush office, considering the condition of the outside, and closed the door behind them. He planted himself firmly in front of the door, arms crossed on his chest. The chair behind the desk swiveled around.

"So, it *is* true. The Baloney Man is back." A tall Hispanic man rose from behind the desk, his hand extended to Dylan. "Been a long time."

Dylan returned the shake. "It sure has."

Ramon motioned for the women to sit down. "What can I do for you?"

"We need a new ID fast," Dylan told him.

"I've already given you one, man."

"Not for me. For her," Dylan pointed out Felicia.

"Sharp looking, lady. You need a job, Sweetheart?" Felicia frowned and looked away.

"Just the ID, Ramon."

"Driver's license or the whole package?"

"Just the license." Ramon nodded and moved a book in the bookcase to the right of his desk. This caused the mirrored wall behind the desk to swing outward. He motioned his head toward the opening and led the way down a dark hall that smelled of mildew into a small, cement block room. Inside, sat a young man, greasy hair tied back into a ponytail. He was sitting beside two state-of-the-art computers. He had headphones over his ears and was bobbing along to music while he typed.

Ramon whistled shrilly and told Felicia to stand against the wall. A pretty Hispanic girl in her early twenties entered and quickly went to stand behind a camera. Ramon told Felicia to smile. She glanced sharply at him then stared straight ahead.

"Perfect," Ramon told her. "Sure you don't want a job here, Sweetheart? Lucy could show you the ropes." Lucy, the girl behind the camera, looked Felicia over disdainfully before disappearing through a door. "This will only take a minute to develop and Hacker here will take care of the DMV files and Marie Ashton will have been born."

"Marie Ashton?" Felicia asked.

"We keep a file of babies that died around the time you were born and we use those names. Less strain on Hacker's brain. He doesn't have to make anything up that way."

"Thanks, Ramon." Dylan shook his hand again. "If we can have our guns back, we'll be on our way."

Natalie handed over the money. "You'll get them on the way out," Ramon told them.

Felicia squinted as they reemerged from the gloomy bar back into the bright sunlight. She frowned and looked at her watch. "Michael is going to be steamed!" she exclaimed. "We've been gone for over an hour!"

"We'll just sneak in the back of the store and act like we've been shopping there the whole time," Dylan laughed. "Don't worry."

"He's a little bit smarter than that," Felicia retorted.

"Well, he won't have a choice but to accept it," Dylan told her. "What's the worse that can happen? He doesn't talk to us the rest of the day?"

"That would be a blessing," Natalie added. Lisa giggled beside her.

True to his word, Dylan snuck them in the loading door of the store and they began hurriedly tossing items from their lists into shopping carts. Lisa was the first to spot Michael angrily pacing the front of the store. She giggled behind her hand and pointed him out to Natalie. She smiled in return and headed towards the front of the store. Dylan and Felicia pushed their baskets up to the registers at the same time.

"Where have you guys been?" Michael asked angrily as he dumped his groceries onto the counter. "I have been roaming this store for an hour. The manager has approached me several times and I've paged every one of you more than once!"

"Calm down, buddy," Dylan said slapping him on the back. "We've been here. Didn't hear the page."

Michael swore and stalked out of the store. He was waiting in the front seat of the car when the others came out. He stared straight ahead. "I'm not sitting cramped in the back seat with those kids anymore." Dylan winked at the others before they all piled in.

When they arrived back at Dylan's, Michael stormed into the house without offering to help carry the groceries. Felicia watched him hurry into the house, slamming the door shut behind him. "Looks like it worked," Natalie said cheerfully, reaching in to grab a sack. "A peaceful evening ahead."

"I don't understand why the two of you deliberately provoke him," Felicia told her, her own arms loaded down. Lisa ran ahead of them to open the door.

"Because it's fun, dear." Natalie smile broadly. "I realize it's not a very Christian way to act, but Michael's attitude gets to us and it's a rather harmless way to let off steam. We're only teasing him."

"You're not teasing him. You mean every bit of it. I think it would be a lot more peaceful around here if we all tried to get along with him."

"I agree," Dylan said from behind them. "But your mom's way is a lot more fun." Natalie glanced up at Felicia to see how she reacted to Dylan's casual reference to her as mom. Felicia's eyes widened and her mouth tightened, before she walked ahead of them into the house.

She deposited her groceries on the table. "Can you handle this, Natalie? I really need a shower." Natalie nodded and silently watched her disappear down the hall. Dylan noticed the forlorn look on Natalie's face.

"I'm sorry," he told her, drawing her close for a tight hug. "I wasn't thinking."

"It's all right," she told him in a muffled voice. "Someday it'll be easier for her to accept. In the meantime, I'm having a hard time breathing." Dylan laughed and released her.

Felicia went first to her room for a change of clothes before heading to the bathroom. She stopped and listened to Dylan and her mother laughing before she opened the bathroom door. She stood there in horror. Michael stood there clad only in jeans, his hair dripping from its recent washing. On his right shoulder was the tattoo of an L. She gasped and ran from the room. Michael sped after her. "Dylan!" she screamed. Natalie and Dylan bolted from the kitchen as Michael grabbed Felicia from behind. Lisa and Mark screamed.

"Oh, God! Help us," Natalie prayed as she noticed the L.

"Just don't anyone move," Michael warned. "Or I'll break her neck." He put a stranglehold on Felicia.

"No, you won't," Dylan told him. "You need her alive. It'll be your life if you kill her. Remember what you taught me today, Felicia. Keep your wits about you." Felicia's eyes were wide with fright and her breathing was fast. Her gaze locked with Dylan's and she nodded. Bringing her foot down forcibly on Michael's, she was able to cause him to loosen his hold on her enough that before he could recover she had flipped him over her shoulder and onto the floor. Dylan quickly jumped him and had him in a headlock. "Quick, Natalie. There's some rope in the closet. Get it." Natalie ran off and returned quickly with it. Dylan dragged Michael over to one of the dining chairs and firmly tied him to it.

Michael began to laugh harshly. "You thought you had us all fooled, you stupid woman!" he told Natalie. "We've known about you from the minute you gave birth."

"How?" she asked, collapsing into a chair.

"Our people started the fire that burned your house. We knew you weren't in it. It was only a matter of time before we had tracked down all the people in your life you still had contact with. We have enough people that it didn't take us long," He laughed again. "And it was me that killed that nosy old woman." Dylan punched him in the face, causing the chair to fall backwards. Michael lay there, his lip bleeding, still laughing.

Felicia put her hands over her ears and shook her head. "No. It's not possible." Tears streamed down her face. "Michael, we grew up together." Michael's laughter increased in volume.

"Shut up!" Dylan yelled, kicking him in the stomach. Lisa screamed again and threw herself to the floor. Mark sat beside her and put his thin arms around her. Dylan seemed to notice the children for the first time and with great difficulty restrained himself from kicking Michael again. "Natalie, you and Felicia start packing. I'll load up the car. We're getting out of here." Dylan grabbed Felicia by the shoulders and shook her. "Felicia! You can't fall apart now. Honey, we have to work together. I need you to pack yours, Natalie's and the children's things while Natalie gets the food. All right?" She nodded numbly and walked slowly to their room, avoiding Michael's gaze. Dylan squatted down before the two children. "Mark, I need your help. I need you to watch Michael and send your sister out after me if he makes a single move. Can you do that?" Mark nodded and fixed his eyes on Michael's. Dylan patted Lisa's head and tilted her face up to his. He kissed her forehead to reassure her and headed outside. They could hear him whistle for the dogs.

"Hey, kid," Michael called to him, spitting blood on the floor. "Come help me up. You don't want to stick around with these guys. Come untie me and I'll show you a wonderful life. I bet I can even find your folks. What about it?" Mark shook his head no. Michael let loose with a string of obscenities and spit again.

Natalie came up behind them and kicked him in the leg. "Leave him alone. I knew I should have ditched you right off."

"You are going to die, woman," Michael told her laughing. "You and that macho cop out there. Luther only cares about Felicia."

"Maybe so," she answered. "But I'm going to a better place when I die. I'm not afraid to die."

"You should be," Michael warned her. "You really should be. Luther can make dying *very* unpleasant."

Felicia walked out with their bags and Natalie followed her outside with the food. Before closing the door behind her, she glanced back at Michael, who grinned evilly. "Come on, kids." Mark and Lisa followed her, carefully scooting around Michael, who made as if to lunge after them. Lisa shrieked and broke into a run. They could hear Michael laughing as they hurried down the front steps.

"What are the horses for?" Natalie asked, noticing the horse trailer hitched to the back of the Bronco.

"We may have to leave the road after a time," Dylan explained. "The dogs are in the back. Put the rest of the stuff in and around them. Anywhere it'll fit. We may be a little cramped but I don't see any way around it right now." Dylan sprinted for the house and hurriedly grabbed some of his own things from his room. He pulled his rifle from over the fireplace and shotgun shells from the top shelf of the closet. The shells went into the bag he had slung over his shoulder and he went to stand over Michael.

"You are all going to die," Michael taunted. Dylan lifted the rifle and brought the barrel down forcibly on Michael's head.

"Sleep tight, buddy." Dylan ran back to the car and jumped in. He sat silently behind the wheel for a few seconds and looked back at his house.

"Dylan?" Natalie said. "I'm sorry." She felt overwhelmed with guilt over dragging Dylan into their circumstances. She tried to think of ways she could have avoided doing so. Maybe if she had disappeared altogether. Then Alice wouldn't be dead and Dylan wouldn't be running from his home with the responsibility of two women and a couple of kids. She sighed deeply. Maybe she should have turned Felicia over to the adoption authorities and went back to Luther, telling him that their daughter have died in childbirth. She knew that he would probably have killed her, but maybe he wouldn't have been able to track down their daughter. She shook her head. Hindsight was accomplishing nothing.

Dylan heard her and nodded. He turned the key in the ignition and drove down the drive, not looking back anymore.

"Where are we going?" Felicia asked.

Dylan shrugged. "I think tonight I'll just find us an out of the way place to camp and try to come up with a plan. If Michael has already contacted his people they'll come looking for him when they don't hear from him. I figure we have at least a day before that happens. I'm not really sure."

Natalie tried shifting to a more comfortable position, wedged as she was in the back seat with two kids and two large dogs heads hanging over the back. She wriggled around and pulled the two children's heads over onto each shoulder. They smiled sleepily up at her before closing their eyes. She stared out the window.

Dylan left Interstate 5 and drove onto Highway 20, keeping to the back roads until they were in the Mendocino National Forest. He had camped here many times before and was familiar with the territory. He knew of places that few campers knew of. He drove the car in as far as the roads would allow and cut off the ignition. He glanced in the rearview mirror and saw that Natalie and the children had fallen asleep. He let his head fall back against the headrest and let it roll over until he could see Felicia. She was silently watching him. He put his right hand up and tenderly cupped her cheek. She leaned into it and smiled wearily. Dylan slid his hand around to the back of her neck and pulled her closer to him, laying her head on his shoulder. They sat that way for several minutes, listening to the sounds of the insects in the forest around them. Away from street and city lights, the night was ink black around them, the tall trees cutting off any light from the moon and stars. Dylan felt her shiver and, sliding around until his back was against the doorframe, placed both his arms around her.

"I've never run from a fight before," he told her quietly. "I've been afraid before. Deathly so, and I've never run. I've always stood my ground and faced my fear and the danger. But... When I realized how Michael had betrayed you and that because of your trust in him your life was in danger, I didn't think twice about getting you out of there. All I could think about was the safety of you, Natalie and those two kids. Its strange having other lives dependent on me. It was only my sister and I for a few years, and I failed to keep her safe. I know that as a police officer, people depend on me all the time, but they're strangers, you know? Not people I've known all my life and care about. After Susan was killed... That's when I became an officer. I wanted to try to keep others from falling into the same trap she did."

Knowing that Dylan was speaking from the heart, Felicia stayed quietly in his arms, amazed at how safe and comfortable she felt there. She had never felt like this with Michael. She rubbed Dylan's arm contemplatively with her hand. "Dylan?" she asked him. "Do you believe in God?"

"Now *that* I struggle with."

"So you're not a Christian?"

"Guess not. Never really took the time to think about it. Why?"

Felicia murmured drowsily, falling asleep listening to Dylan's heartbeat. "I can't fall in love with someone who's not a Christian." Dylan softly placed a kiss on the top of her head and laid his own back against the window. He sat silently staring into the night.

Chapter 9

"I have to go to the bathroom," Lisa whined the next morning.

Natalie forced her eyes open against the glare of the morning sun and put a finger up to her lips. She looked in the front seat and saw that Dylan and Felicia were still asleep. She struggled to sit upright after sleeping in such a cramped position and tried to quietly open the door. Immediately, the two dogs' heads poked over the back of the seat.

"Come on," she whispered to them and they bounded over the seat and outside, waking Mark. He groaned and sat up, rubbing the sleep from his eyes. "We'll go over there into the trees to use the restroom," Natalie told them, leading them away from the Bronco. "Mark, you turn around until we're finished and then it'll be your turn."

The cool breeze from the open door woke Dylan and Felicia. She sat up, feeling a little self-conscious in the light of the morning. Pulling away from Dylan, she noticed that Natalie and the children were gone. She bolted from the car, Dylan quickly following.

"Natalie!" Felicia called in alarm.

"We're right here," Natalie called back. "We had to take a nature break." Felicia sighed in relief and gathered the children close for a hug.

"Where are the dogs?" Dylan asked.

"Doing the same as us, I suspect." Natalie glanced back. "I'll see what I can dig up for breakfast." She climbed up into the back of the car and began rummaging in the boxes they had brought. "We left in such a hurry, there's not much to choose from," she told them, handing out a bag of apples. "I did manage to grab these." She handed one out to everyone. "Dylan, do you think we could manage another trip into town?"

He nodded and whistled for the dogs. Instantly, he was answered with barks as the dogs came bounding from the bushes, prancing and jumping around him. He laughed and patting their heads, ordered them back into the car. "Need a nature break?" he asked Felicia. She shook her head and smiled, embarrassed.

"Okay," Dylan said when they were back on the road. "Felicia, make a list of what we need. We're going to be roughing it quite a bit." He thought for a minute. "We'll need a tent. Big enough for all of us. Food for the dogs and horses. Food for us. Maybe another gun, a knife, and definitely ammunition. Sleeping bags, warm clothing, flashlights and some heavy coats. The further north we get, the colder it'll be. Natalie? Can you handle this financially?" She nodded and patted the bag on the floor next to her feet. "I figure we'll make camp in the forest, maybe up around Ferndale and take it easy for a few days. Try to get our bearings and come up with a plan."

The kids chattered non-stop on the drive to a little town on the outskirts of Sacramento. The group stopped at a small roadside café for breakfast. The café was a rustic building made of plank siding, complete with blue and white-checkered French café curtains on the windows and booth cushions. Mark and Lisa sniffed appreciatively as they walked through the front door. "All right!" Mark exclaimed. "Pancakes!" The kids could barely contain their excitement as they waited for the hostess to seat them. The cafe was on a back road out of the main tourist stream and was only half filled with customers. Dylan glanced around, and not noting anyone paying them overdue attention, relaxed and took his seat in the booth.

Natalie exhaled and leaned back. The kids ate the pancakes with gusto, and she smiled as she watched them. Dylan and Felicia talked quietly, their heads bent towards each other. She sighed and straightened up, digging into her own breakfast of eggs and bacon.

It was a Saturday and the sporting goods store was packed with people. Natalie grabbed the hands of both children and Dylan took Felicia's arm. "Let's hurry with our shopping," he told them. "I don't feel comfortable with this many people." They took turns trying on hiking boots and the kids ran in and out of the tents that were on display. Felicia checked off each item as it was placed in their basket. As Dylan was lacing up a pair of the hiking boots on Felicia's feet, he happened to glance over her shoulder and noticed a young man with a shaved head wearing a black leather jacket, staring at them. Dylan returned the stare but the other man did not lower his eyes or move to leave. He quietly told Felicia and the others that it was time to go. "Just wear the boots out of the store," he told Felicia. "I'll hand the empty box to the cashier." They hurriedly paid for their purchases and headed further into town before stopping at a discount department store.

Dylan told them to only purchase enough clothing for a few days. Dylan followed behind them as the women loaded the shopping cart with clothing and paper products. He kept an eye in all directions, looking for the young man they had seen at the sporting goods store. Not seeing him, Dylan breathed a sigh of relief and waited off to the side as Natalie paid. "One more stop," he told them, "and we're off to find a campsite." At the grocery store, they loaded up with bottled water and non-perishable foods. Forgetting something on the next aisle, Felicia turned the corner and found herself face to face with the young man from the sporting goods store. He stood stiffly before her, unsmiling. He reached out to grab her arm and she quickly turned and ran back to the group. When she looked back over her shoulder, he was gone. She told Dylan what had happened and without further delay he rushed the group outside and into the car. Once everyone was safely inside, he turned angrily to Felicia. "What were you doing off on you own?" he demanded.

"I forgot something," she said defensively.

"I can't watch you every single second. There's too many of us." Dylan's mouth was set in a grim line. "I've got to depend on you to be responsible enough to stay together!"

"I'm sorry!" she retorted. "Nothing happened!"

"It could have!"

"Well, it didn't. They wouldn't grab me in a crowded public place anyway." She sat back against the back of her seat.

Dylan started the car. "People disappear from crowded places all the time."

"Dylan's right, Felicia," Natalie added from the back seat. "We've all got to be careful. *Especially* you. You're the one Luther really wants. The rest of us are expendable."

Felicia sighed and turned to stare out the window. Dylan squealed tires out of the parking lot and headed back to the forest. The ride was made mostly in silence. Occasionally the children would say something as they played hand games, and Natalie spent the time quietly reading her bible. Felicia sat staring out the passenger window, speaking only when someone spoke to her. Although her physical demeanor didn't soften as she watched the beautiful scenery roll by, her spirit was soothed. She hummed hymns under her breath.

Dylan drove down roads that were barely more than paths, and some of the holes he hit caused those in the back seat to bounce high enough to hit their heads on their roof. At one point the bouncing was so severe that the dogs whined in protest. Finally, Dylan stopped and everyone crawled painfully from the car.

"No one can find us here," Lisa stated. "We're out in the middle of nowhere."

"Don't be silly," Mark told her. "If we can find this place, so can someone else. Right, Dylan?"

Dylan laid a hand on Mark's shoulder. "You're pretty wise for one so young. Yes. Someone else could find us if they looked hard enough." Dylan whistled for the dogs to come back after they had disappeared into the thick foliage. He commanded them to stay. "Well, let's start getting this thing unloaded." He popped the hatch on the back of the car and then started pulling out supplies and placing them on the ground. "I'll set up the tent," he told them, "and the food needs to go back in the car. There's a creek right down that path. Felicia, take Mark with you and get some water." She glared at him. Grabbing the bucket, she set off towards the creek.

"Don't be mad at him," Mark said once they were away from the others. "I think he really likes you. He's just worried."

Felicia smiled sheepishly down at him and ruffled his hair. "You're right. I've been acting more like I'm Lisa's age than my own haven't I?" She reached down and took the boy's hand. "I'm glad he sent you with me. You're good for me." Mark grinned proudly and took the bucket from her.

Felicia inhaled deeply, filling her lungs with the fresh mountain air. She stopped in the center of the path and looked up into the tall trees. The foliage was so thick that sunlight barely broke through. Ahead, they could hear the gurgling of a small stream. "I feel like skipping. Can you skip?"

"Skipping is for girls."

"Not really. How about singing? Do you like to sing?"

Mark shook his head. "I really haven't had a chance to sing much."

"I'll show you how much fun it can be." She started singing a silly child song, and Mark found himself giggling. While she sang, the two skipped down the path until they reached the stream. They could faintly hear the murmuring of Natalie and Dylan as they set up camp. A sudden crashing in the brush behind them caused Felicia to scream and jump back in alarm. Within seconds, Duke came bounding out on the path beside them.

"You silly dog," Mark scolded. "You scared her."

"Scared me, huh? You weren't scared?" Felicia teased.

Mark hid his face in the dog's neck. "Of course not," he mumbled.

"Right." Felicia laughed and dipped the bucket into the stream. She then sat the full bucket on the bank and pulled off her shoes.

"Come on, Mark. Let's wade." She rolled up the legs of her jeans and walked into the water. "Oooh! It's cold!" Mark laughed, yanked off his own shoes, and hurried in after her. Duke stood on the stream bank and barked at the antics of the two as they shrieked and splashed each other. They all looked up in surprise as Dylan came running down the path, gun in hand.

"What?" Felicia stood before him, her hair and clothes dripping.

"What's going on?" Dylan asked panting, resting his hands on his knees.

Mark stood still and let the water swirl around his legs. "We're just playing."

"I heard screaming and the dog barking," Dylan explained between breaths. "I got worried." He smiled at his own nervousness. He was both relieved and happy that they could find time to have fun in the midst of their troubles. Putting down his gun, he ran into the water, sending big splashes out around him. Felicia and Mark shrieked and tried to run. Dylan caught Felicia by the shoulders and put his leg behind her knee, then pulled her back until she was submerged. Mark laughed and splashed Dylan. Dylan let the sputtering Felicia up and laughed again. "Guess I'll go back to camp and get Natalie and Lisa. This is a perfect place for a picnic." He shoved Felicia's wet hair back from her face, leaving her standing there, mouth open in astonishment.

When Dylan returned later with Natalie and Lisa they found Felicia and Mark dozing in the sun by the stream. Felicia's long hair was fanned out around her as it dried. Her lashes left shadows on her pale cheeks. "She's beautiful, isn't she?" Natalie asked Dylan.

Dylan continued to stare down at her and nodded. "Absolutely," he whispered.

"Like a fairy princess," Lisa added.

Dylan laughed softly. "Couldn't have said it better myself. What do you say we wake them?" He took a paper cup from the bag they had brought with them and filled it with cold water from the creek. He dumped it on the sleeping two and jumped back. Felicia sat up shrieking and Mark laughed. Natalie shook off the blanket and began setting out the food while Felicia scolded Dylan.

"I was dry!"

"Not anymore," he told her, ducking as she threw the cup at him.

"I'm starved!" Mark told them hurriedly putting on his shoes.

"You're always starved!" Lisa said, pushing him. "Move over and let me get on the blanket."

"Come on you two," Felicia said. "There's plenty of room. It's a beautiful day. We've got a lovely lunch, so let's not spoil it by fighting." She looked up into the blue sky. They sat in a small clearing by the tall redwoods of Northern California. "Look up," she told them. "It's like a wonderful cathedral of God and if we're really quiet, we can hear the angels singing." The group sat quietly and Felicia fought back a smile at the serious expressions on the children's faces as they strained to hear music. Birds twittered gaily in the trees and the wind whispered teasingly through the branches. "Can you hear it? Even the wind praises the Lord."

"I can only hear birds," Lisa stated, shoving a cookie in her mouth.

"How can the wind praise?" Mark asked skeptically.

"The bible says that even the trees and rocks worship the one who created them. Isn't that amazing?"

"Kind of hard to believe." Mark stuffed a sandwich in his mouth.

"I'm with you." Dylan had been watching Felicia rather than the trees and birds. He had seen too much of the evil in life to easily accept the notion of a loving God. "It's kind of hard to believe."

Felicia looked over at him and frowned. "How can you sit out here within the beauty of nature and doubt for a minute that a loving hand created it all? Everything has a purpose and a beauty all its own."

"I haven't seen a lot of beauty in my life," he told her. "I'm sitting here looking at one of the most beautiful creations *I've* ever seen." He winked at her. "Maybe there's hope for me after all."

"Dylan, really!"

"Okay," he said becoming serious. "You want to talk about this now. We will. I've seen a lot of senseless killing. Kids being shot down in the streets. People dying of horrible, debilitating diseases. I've seen the filth of the ghetto and the hopelessness on those people's faces. I've seen homeless people freeze to death in their sleep. I've seen people fall and pass out in their own waste. Where's the beauty in that, Felicia? Tell me!" He crumpled up his soda can. "Where was the hand of God when my sister was sacrificed like an animal or when my aunt was butchered in her own kitchen?" Dylan was becoming angry.

Felicia's eyes swelled with tears. "I loved Honey, too. I will miss her every day of my life. God didn't kill her, Dylan. Someday we'll see the reason for her dying. I can't imagine living without the hope and knowledge of a God who loves me."

"Yeah! Right! God didn't kill her, but he sure allowed it to happen." Dylan threw the uneaten portion of his sandwich down and stood up. "I'll be back at the car if you guys need anything." He stalked off. Mark copied him by throwing down his own sandwich and followed him.

Lisa had sat wide-eyed during the fiery exchange and once Dylan and Mark left, the little girl scooted closer to Felicia and lay her head in her lap. "I believe in God," she whispered. Felicia smiled and smoothed back the little girl's hair.

"Don't worry, honey," Natalie told her reaching over and taking her hand. "He'll come around. Dylan has a big heart, but he's stubborn and he's dealing with a lot of anger. He'll have to find God the hard way and in his own time."

Felicia nodded and absently sat smoothing Lisa's hair until the child fell asleep. The last couple of days had put her on a roller coaster of emotions. She felt like a small ship being tossed to and fro on a stormy sea. She was used to peaceful and carefree days. She had been safe in the sureness of Honey and God's love. Her faith had wavered a bit over these last few days. She smiled sadly down at the sleeping girl and gently laid her back on the blanket. She glanced over at her mother. Natalie's eyes were wide and she was gasping for air.

"What?!" she asked, frightened.

"He's coming," Natalie whispered, panicking. "I can feel him."

"How do you know?" Felicia asked alarmed. "Is he coming now?"

Natalie shook her head. "Not today. Maybe not tomorrow... but he's following us and he's getting closer."

Felicia looked up the path in the direction Dylan and Mark had taken. "What do we do?"

"Keep running."

Back at camp, Dylan had tethered the horses to the trees and was busily cleaning out the horse trailer. He didn't notice that Mark had followed him and was startled to find the boy staring at him when he turned around. He forced a smile to his lips. "Hey, sport.

Who's watching the girls?"

Mark shrugged. "I wanted to come with you. Not stuck back there with the girls."

Dylan nodded with understanding. "Well, then you can help me." Dylan handed him a broom. "Sweep this trailer out for me, will you? I'm going to take a look at this map." Dylan retrieved a map of Northern California from his back pocket and spread it out on the hood of the Bronco. They were camped in the Mendocino National Forest off the Redding Bypass Road. He chewed his inner lip as he studied the surrounding roads. Alone, he would have chosen to confront Luther right away and head on, but having the women and children with him cause enough to slow down and contemplate hiding for a while. Taking his time and stopping at small, populated towns along the way. He knew they could hide quite a while in the Trinity Alps or Marble Mountains, but the nights were only getting colder. Felicia and Natalie weren't ready for a confrontation with Luther yet. He made the decision to stay where they were for another night or two and then continue along Vestal road to the nearest town. Maybe a night at a bed-and-breakfast would lighten everyone's mood.

"How's this?" Mark called, interrupting Dylan's thoughts.

"Looks great."

"Can I do anything else? Maybe help you come up with a plan?" The boy hopped down from the trailer. "I'm really smart."

Dylan laughed. "I'm sure you are. What makes you think I'm coming up with a plan?"

"Cops always have some kind of a plan."

"You watch too much TV. I don't have much of a plan yet." Dylan folded the map. "We're going to stay here at least for tonight and slowly work our way north. Sound okay to you?"

Mark nodded. They were interrupted by the sounds of the women returning. Mark turned to greet them while Dylan stashed the map in the glove compartment. Behind the seat, he withdrew a couple of fishing poles. "How about the two of us go fishing?" Mark's face lit up and he eagerly followed Dylan back down the path. Dylan avoided Felicia's eyes as they passed. She bit her bottom lip and turned to

Natalie.

"I really managed to make him mad at me." She tossed her head in the direction Dylan had taken.

"You're like salt in a raw wound. God's been working on that man for a while." Natalie stashed the leftover picnic in the back of the car. "Dylan likes to deny the existence of God, but then at other times, he blames God."

"I don't understand." Felicia opened the door to the car and sat inside, dangling her legs out the door.

"Well… You know that his sister was involved in the same cult I was. She was young and pretty. Luther sacrificed her during one of his rituals. Dylan didn't find her in time to save her. He has never forgiven himself for that. Says God could have saved her if He was real." Natalie leaned back against the car. "I've tried explaining things to him several times, but right now he's not buying it. Wouldn't even listen when Alice tried." She shrugged. "Let's get the bedding laid out in the tent. Hopefully we'll have fish for breakfast in the morning. Either way, it'll be late when the guys return."

It was getting to be dusk by the time Dylan and Mark returned. Dylan had several fish in water in the bucket and set about stringing the bucket up in a tree. Mark proceeded to tell the girls several whopping fish stories. Dylan looked over and caught Felicia's eye. "I'm sorry," he mouthed. She smiled back at him and carried the lantern over.

"Forgiven."

Dylan took the lantern from her and hung it from a low tree branch. "Tired?" he asked her. She nodded and he put his arm around her, pulling her close. "I'll try not to get so carried away when you bring up God. I know he's important to you."

Later that night, Dylan sat up abruptly in his sleeping bag. The dogs lay by his side, growling low in their throats, the hair standing on the nape of their necks. He shushed them and listened. He could hear the crunching of dead leaves outside their tent and occasionally huffing. Slowly, he withdrew his pistol from beside him.

"What is it?" Felicia asked, quietly.

Dylan put his finger to his lips and crawled cautiously to the tent opening. As he reached out to pull aside the flap, he fell backward and yelled in surprise as the head of a large black bear was thrust its head through the doorway. Felicia scrambled back, desperately trying to free herself from her sleeping bag and woke up Lisa who sat up screaming. The bear roared and withdrew as both dogs launched themselves at it. Natalie sat up and hurriedly motioned for Felicia to watch the children, and grabbing her own gun, rushed outside with Dylan.

The bear was standing on his hind legs several feet from the tent. He swayed his head back and forth, sniffing the air. As the dogs rushed closer and ran in circles around him, the bear lowered once again to all fours and with ears laid flat against his head, began slapping its front feet against the ground. The horses were shrieking and straining at their tethers off to one side as Dylan yelled for Felicia.

She left the children inside the tent and crawled cautiously out. "Hold the horses!" Dylan ordered her. "See if you can't calm them down before they hurt themselves." He ordered the dogs to back down as the bear stood upright again and roared.

"What do we do?" Natalie asked, fear showing across her face. "Do you want me to shoot it?"

"Not if we don't have to! We probably wouldn't kill it and a wounded bear is extremely dangerous. I think maybe he's just curious. It's the dogs that are annoying him! Duke! Luke! Step down!" The dogs looked back at the bear and, still growling low in their throats, came to stand beside Dylan. Felicia had the horses' reins and was struggling to hold them as they reared in terror.

"Natalie! Wave your arms and yell. Be aggressive. Don't let him think you're prey. Make yourself bigger than you are." Dylan began to wave his arms over his head and yell. The bear dropped back to all fours and roared again, tossing his head from side to side. Surprisingly fast, the animal charged towards the tent, swiping it with one huge paw. The two children inside screamed as the tent collapsed on top of them. Dylan yelled again and fired his gun over the bear's head. The animal roared once more and lumbered back off into the forest.

Dylan watched him go then hurried over to relieve Felicia as Natalie began unburying the children from the tattered tent.

"Was he after the fish?" Felicia asked as Dylan took the horses and began calming them.

"Maybe. And maybe he was just curious." Dylan stroked the neck of one of the horses, and the animal's muscles were quivering nervously under its skin. "With all the camping now, bears just aren't as afraid of people as they once were." He smiles over at her. "I guess we'll go back to sleeping cramped in the car."

Felicia smiled back. "Good idea."

Chapter 10

Luther's car stopped on the bank of a lake and the driver got out to open the door for him. Waiting in the water just a few feet away, was a small motor-powered boat. The two silently got in the boat and Luther was driven to an island in the center of the lake. He looked with pride on the buildings built on the island. His world! He was the lord here! Several smaller buildings surrounded an even smaller one in the center. Luther worked at keeping his small community running smoothly while maintaining a look of abandonment to the casual observer. The center building, and most of the living quarters, was built underground, with only the entrances above ground. The center building was where Luther held his worship meetings and rituals. As the boat neared the shore, people scurried from the buildings and hurried to the center hall. Luther smiled in satisfaction. His people were trained well. They knew their leader, and obeyed. If they didn't, they paid a severe penalty for their disobedience.

Luther exited the boat smoothly and walked leisurely into the building where the others had already gathered. Over two hundred adults were gathered there to greet him on his return. "The Children of Light" had few children of their own and these few children were kept hidden away and trained quietly in the ways of the people.

Luther stood behind a wooden podium set up on a platform. He rested his hands on each side and leaned forward. "We've found them," he said quietly. Two hundred heads nodded in unison. "They are hiding in the Mendocino National Forest. I want them caught and brought here. Mainly…the girl. Also the children, if you can achieve it. You can kill the rest. They are of no real use to us. A great reward awaits the ones who succeeds in this." For several seconds, Luther stared out over the crowd. Without another word, he disappeared behind a black curtain. Silently, the others withdrew and the men left in small groups to cross over the lake.

Luther entered a small room. In it was a single chair set before another black curtain. He pulled the curtain aside to reveal a one-way mirror. He smiled and seated himself in the chair. With his hands folded under his chin, he silently watched the young girls on the other side. They were totally oblivious to his presence. The room where they were kept was fairly sparse. The marble tile was white and the walls matched the white hue exactly. Blankets were piled neatly in one corner of the room. There were no beds, no chairs and no pillows. Luther wanted his people to learn self-denial and discipline. When someone entered into his commune they entered into a vow of poverty and unity and turned over all their worldly goods to the community fund.

He could hear the girls weeping and he fed on their fear. Many of the girls who disappeared in the surrounding towns ended up here, in Luther's world. He kept them strictly for ritual purposes and enjoyed indulging himself in their fright. Luther practiced only abstinence now, as was befitting his role as high priest. He kept himself pure as he ordered his people to do. The exceptional girls were used to increase his population with the men in his high order, but they were usually girls of high beauty and intelligence. For now, Luther only watched. The one he wanted would soon be with him.

He smiled and almost laughed out loud when one of his men entered the room on the other side of the glass and the girls screamed in horror. Luther demanded that his people wear hideous masks when they entered the captives' room. He wanted his captives afraid. They were easier to control when they were afraid. The man who entered the room carried a small whip and would occasionally strike one of the girls if they were too slow to move out of his way. He carried a large bowl of oatmeal and set it in the center of the floor. The girls stayed against the wall until he was gone and then swarmed the bowl, using their hands to shove the food in their mouth. Luther smiled again and closed the curtain. There were other things to attend to. His own pleasure would have to wait.

Adjacent to the room where Luther sat was his home and office. It was a small room with a curtain partitioning off the bathroom. A narrow bed was placed against one wall. A table with two chairs sat pushed up against the opposite wall. Luther's needs were few and he required little sleep. On the table sat a phone, which Luther picked up and punched in a number. Within seconds, there was a knock on his door.

Two men entered. Luther motioned with his head for one of them to sit across the table from him while the other took up a position by the door. "I trust everything was in order during my absence," he told them.

The man across the table was large with a shaved head. Scars ran up and down his arms from the colorful tattoos that Luther had ordered him to have removed. He did not allow his people to paint themselves with make-up or any other artificiality. The man stared vacantly ahead, not daring to meet Luther's eyes. To have eye contact was to put yourself on an equal footing with Luther and this was strictly forbidden.

"One of the prisoners tried to escape," the man said woodenly.

Luther folded his hands tightly in front of him. The only other sign of his anger was the white skin around his knuckles. "And how, exactly, is this possible?"

The man flinched slightly under Luther's cold stare. "He was teasing them, sir."

"Teasing them? How?"

The man swallowed. Luther smiled at his nervousness. "He was tearing at their clothes, sir."

"Trying to defile them?" Luther put his fingertips together under his chin. "These girls are not here for the people's pleasure. Some of them are to be used in a sacred way." His eyes glinted. "Send this imbecile to the square." The man nodded and silently the two men left the room.

The square was simply a log cemented into a square of concrete in the middle of Luther's community. The accused was tied to the post with his hands above his head and facing out towards the crowd. Someone else was ringing a bell, signaling the commune to gather. Luther stood calmly beside the accused until everyone was gathered and was silent. He spoke quietly and calmly. "This man has chosen to disobey the rules of our community. He chose to do so while I was away. He must be punished as an example of my supreme authority and to discourage others who may be tempted to follow his disobedience." Luther's voice began to rise in volume and boomed across the courtyard. "Is there anyone here who disagrees with me?" He looked over to where a woman stood, tears silently coursing down her face. The tears were her only sign of emotion. "Good."

Quickly, Luther withdrew a sharp dagger and slit the man's throat. He then handed the weapon to the crying woman. She nodded and withdrew from the crowd. She knew what was expected of her. Later, when she was alone in her room, she was to silently use the knife on herself. This was to atone for the disobedience of her mate. After handing the woman the knife, Luther walked back to his room. The men, who had earlier visited Luther in his room, cut the dead man down and dragged him away. No one had spoken or made any other sound while Luther had carried out the man's punishment.

Chapter 11

The man hiding in the bushes near the Bronco, watched silently as the group ate the fish Dylan and Mark had caught the evening before. He was excited, thinking about his reward when he returned to Luther with the woman. Discipline was harsh among the people, but the rewards were sweet and worth the risks. He knew that his first concern was to disable the man with them. He didn't consider the women and children a threat. He looked around him nervously. Now, if only he could find the dogs. He couldn't see them, so he listened carefully. He could hear a faint bark. Good, they were a ways off. He stepped from his hiding place, and ducking down, snuck quietly around the vehicle.

Dylan leaned back against a tree trunk, comfortably full. He almost regretted the fact that he had quit smoking a few months ago. Relaxing moments like these made the desire for a cigarette strong. "I cook a really mean fish," he boasted, laughing.

"My fish was bigger than yours!" Mark protested.

Dylan winked at him. "That was supposed to be our secret, buddy. My ego is bigger than yours."

Natalie laughed and crawled around the blanket they had spread on the ground, cleaning up after their meal. Lisa looked up and screamed as a man ran towards them, a knife clutched tightly in his hand. Dylan leaped to his feet and shoved Felicia behind him. "Mark! Get your sister and run! Run into the trees and find the dogs!" Mark grabbed Lisa's hand and together they tore off through the brush, frantically calling for the dogs.

"I just want the woman," the man told them. "The rest of you can go."

Dylan was careful to keep himself between this man and the others. "I don't think so. No one is going anywhere with you." The two men began circling each other and Dylan motioned for Felicia to step back and join the others.

"I'm taking her with me now, or I'll take your life."

"You'll kill me anyway. I might as well die fighting."

"Please, God," Felicia began to pray.

"Sorry. I'm afraid I can't let you have her." Dylan glanced towards the Bronco, where his gun was. He knew the distance was too far to try running for it. Pushing backwards, he shoved Felicia into the nearby bushes and then lunged towards the stranger. Natalie screamed his name and then turned to run to the car. She could hear the shuffles and grunts as the two men grappled. Desperately she searched underneath the rear seat for her bag. She glanced back to see the two men roll under the horses' feet, causing the horses to rear and scream in terror. The horses strained at their tethers, trying desperately to dance around the fighting men and avoid stepping on them.

Although Dylan was a tall man, the attacker was even taller and wider in the body. Dylan concentrated on staying away from the knife the man wielded wildly. The attacker's eyes shone as if with an artificial light and the wicked smile on his lips never faded. Not even when Dylan managed to land a solid punch to his jaw. Dylan jumped back as the knife tore through his shirt, narrowly missing his skin. He could hear Felicia yelling to Natalie and had to force himself to stay focused on the man before him, not on the two women. They would be in danger if he was overcome and they were left alone.

Tears were streaming down Natalie's cheeks by the time she found her gun and her breath was coming in hard little gasps. She fumbled at the bottom of her purse for her extra bullets. She kept the gun unloaded since they had gotten the children and her hands shook as she tried to grasp the little cylinders. She looked up, startled as the other door to the vehicle was wrenched open.

"Hurry!" Felicia ordered harshly. "Dylan needs our help and I don't know what to do!" She disappeared again. Felicia ran over to where the two men were struggling and glanced furiously around the ground. Spying a large rock, she grabbed it and drew back her arm to throw it. If only they weren't moving so fast! She was afraid of hitting Dylan and tried desperately to calm herself. There! She let fly with the rock. The attacker yelped as the rock caught him squarely in the back and for a moment his attention was diverted. Dylan lunged at his legs, knocking him once again to the ground. They grappled together, each man taking turns having the advantage. Dylan could feel himself beginning to tire. He fell back as he heard the report of Natalie's gun and as the attacker fell forward onto him, the blade from the man's knife plunged into Dylan's shoulder.

Natalie stood a few feet from them, her legs spaced wide apart, her breathing still fast. The tears had dried, leaving tracks in the dust. Their attacker lay unmoving where Dylan had tossed him off himself. Dylan struggled to his feet and looked around for Felicia. She stood, eyes wide, staring at her mother. He moved clumsily to Natalie's side and gently removed the gun from her grasp.

"I've never killed anyone before," she whispered.

"And we don't know if you've killed anyone now. Either way, it was him or me, if that makes you feel any better." He put the gun on the hood of the Bronco and walked over to where their assailant lay. By this time, the children and dogs had returned. Mark was visibly relieved when he saw that the fallen man wasn't Dylan and he ran to try and calm the panicking horses. Dylan felt for the man's pulse. "He's still alive. Felicia, get me the rope from the back of the trailer." When she didn't move, he ordered again. "Felicia! The rope!" Beads of sweat had begun forming on Dylan's forehead and upper lip. He drew in a deep breath to try and still the dizziness that was rapidly coming over him. His vision was becoming blurred and he stood still, blinking. As Felicia handed him the rope, she noticed the unusual pallor of his skin and became aware of the blood soaking through his shirt.

"Dylan, you're hurt!"

He shook his head and collapsed to the ground, clutching his chest. "Something... on the... knife. I can't... breathe." He closed his eyes.

"Natalie! Help me!" Felicia screamed. "Dylan's been stabbed!"

Natalie rushed over to where Felicia sat leaning over Dylan. She ripped the fabric of his sleeve away from the wound. The injury was a more of a puncture than a cut and was bleeding profusely. She used the torn-away sleeve to make a tourniquet. "We've got to get him to a doctor."

"My…wallet. Doctor Walsh. Take… me… there."

Felicia rolled him over to his side and fished in his pockets until she found his wallet. She searched until she found a small scrap of paper with an address and phone number. "Here it is. He lives outside of San Francisco."

"Mark!" Natalie called. "We're going to need your help. Get the horses loaded into the trailer!" Mark ran over to do as he was told. The dogs were barking furiously and Lisa began to scream as the man Natalie shot began to regain consciousness. "Lisa! Don't just stand there! Shut those dogs up and put them in the car!" Felicia and Natalie both grabbed one of Dylan's arms and slung them around their necks. They struggled under his weight but were finally able to get him into the back seat. Lisa finally got the dogs calmed down and, grabbing hold of their collars, forced them over to the vehicle. Natalie ordered the two children into the back with the dogs so Felicia could have Dylan stretched out on the back seat. She lay his head in her lap and tried to apply pressure to his wound. As she increased the pressure with the heel of her hand, Dylan groaned.

Mark look back to where they had tied up their assailant. "I hope a bear gets him."

Felicia laughed nervously and looked up at Natalie. Natalie smiled wanly back through the rearview mirror. "Let's just leave him to God, okay?" Mark nodded and settled back against the boxes of food, pulling one of the dogs down beside him. He began to absentmindedly stroke the dog's fur.

Felicia sat crying silently as she stared down at Dylan's white face. His breathing was so shallow she could barely see his chest rise and fall.

"How is he?" Natalie asked from the front seat.

"We've got to hurry. Sometimes I can't tell if he's breathing or not." Felicia began to pray silently as she smoothed Dylan's hair back from his face.

Mark and Lisa leaned over the seat. Lisa started to say something and her brother shushed her. "Can't you see that she's praying?" Mark frowned at his sister. "She needs to concentrate."

"You don't need to concentrate to pray."

"Yes, you do!"

"No, you don't!"

"Kids! Please!" Natalie shouted from the front seat. "We're all stressed enough without you two fighting." Lisa stuck her tongue out at her brother and lay back against the rear window.

It was late when they pulled up in front of a small brick house in an older section of San Francisco. The doctor's office was located in the front, with his living quarters in the back. It was beginning to get dark so Natalie switched off the car's lights and drove around to the back of the building. She left the engine running as she hurried up to the door to check whether the doctor was home. She pounded furiously on the door for several seconds before it opened. An older man in his early sixties, wearing sweat pants and a faded T-shirt opened the door. "Yes?"

"Do you know a Dylan Bowen?"

"Why?"

"He's been hurt and he told us to bring him here."

Without further words, the doctor hurried down the steps and to the Bronco. He flung open the door and snapped at Felicia. "What happened?"

"He was stabbed." She slid out and helped the doctor support Dylan's inert form. "After he was stabbed he began to complain about his breathing. Said something was on the knife. We were camping away from…"

"I just need to know how he was hurt. Don't waste my time with any more details than are necessary. Every minute counts." The doctor supported Dylan's weight and as fast as he was able, got Dylan into the house. Natalie and the two children followed close behind. The doctor put Dylan into a small room with a hospital bed and equipment. Within minutes he had Dylan hooked up to oxygen and was cleaning the wound. He looked up, and as if noticing the children for the first time, ordered them out of the room. "This is no place for kids." Natalie took the children out to the waiting room and tried to make them comfortable on a pair of old sofas.

"Doctor," Felicia began. "We need to keep our visit here a secret. Can you do that?"

"Never saw you before." The older man sighed loudly as if annoyed that she felt it necessary to state the obvious. "He's been poisoned with curare, if my guess is correct. It's a South American poison the Indians used to use on their arrows. It's primarily used as an anesthetic now. Harmless, if administered correctly. Incorrectly, it can cause paralysis by blocking neuromuscular activity. Death isn't caused by the poison itself, but rather by asphyxia. This shot of neostigmine should have him as good as new in a few hours. You did well on controlling the bleeding." The doctor injected Dylan with the antidote. He looked up at Felicia. "First thing in the morning, I want all of you out of here. I want no business with these people he's been chasing, or that all of you are running from. I'm helping Dylan because I was a friend of his father's. His father is dead. My loyalty stops there." He wiped his hands off with a white towel and stalked out of the room.

"Good night, doctor," she said quietly, watching his retreating back. "I'll pray for you." She leaned over and planted a gentle kiss on Dylan's forehead.

"How is he?" Natalie asked.

"Dr. Walsh said he'd be all right in the morning. He wants us all out of here first thing."

"I've brought you a blanket. I'll sleep in the waiting room with the kids. Call me if you want me to relieve you."

"I'll be all right. I'd rather be here with him."

Natalie nodded and gave her a quick hug. Felicia pulled up the one chair in the room and placed it next to the bed. She took Dylan's limp hand in hers and watched him sleep.

The sun was just rising the next morning when Dylan opened his eyes. For several seconds he looked around in confusion, not certain of where he was. He tried to rise and winced from the pain in his arm and the IV needle in his hand. He pulled the needle from his hand and tried sitting up again. He stood and grew dizzy. Rather than finding himself in an embarrassing position on the floor, he sat back on the edge of the bed until his wooziness passed. It was then that he noticed Felicia asleep in the chair beside him. He reached over and cupped her cheek with his hand.

"Should you be getting up?" she asked sleepily.

"The good doctor Walsh likes his patients up and out early."

"Do you feel all right to be leaving? We could find a motel."

"Did you sleep in that chair all night?"

"Most of it." She stood and assisted him up from the bed. He stood and swayed, a little unsteady on his feet. Felicia grabbed at him in alarm.

"I'm fine. Just getting my feet back under me." He attempted a few more steps. "What about our friend in the woods?"

"We left him tied to the tree."

Dylan laughed. "A good place for him."

"Mark wanted to leave him as bear food."

Dylan tried to stretch his arm above his head and winced. "Ouch! Guess I'll be crippled for a few days." He reached over and took Felicia's chin in his good hand. "Thanks for sitting up with me." He leaned in to kiss her just as there was a knock on the door and Natalie entered.

"Good. You're up. Your good friend, Doctor Walsh is really anxious to see us leave."

"Then... Let's go." Dylan grabbed what was left of his shirt and started to put it on. Natalie took it from him and handed him a clean shirt, tossing the stained one into a nearby trashcan.

"I'm starved."

"Only a man would get stabbed, nearly die and wake up the next morning thinking about food."

"That's not all I woke up thinking about," he said softly, looking at

Felicia.

She blushed and left the room to get the kids ready.

They didn't see the doctor as they left that morning so Natalie left a few hundred dollars on the examining table. She asked the Lord to bless the old man for his help and hurried outside where the others were waiting for her. She slid in behind the wheel. "I'll drive." Dylan slid into the passenger seat and Felicia got in back with the kids. He pointed the way to a small doughnut shop down the street and Natalie went in alone to get their breakfast.

"It's spooky," Felicia said, watching people walk by the window of the Bronco. "We don't know about anyone. That nice looking man sitting at that table could be looking for us, or that woman over there reading a book. What if those two kids on the motorcycle are looking for us?" She plopped back against her seat. "I don't like feeling this afraid."

"Someday it'll all be behind us," Dylan told her.

"I feel so paranoid."

"That's how you should be feeling. It's safer." He leaned toward the front seat. "Felicia... I mean it. Everyone is suspect. You let your guard down and someone gets killed. We let our guard down back there at camp. We can't let that happen again."

"I was so afraid. Dylan, you could have died and we would have been left alone. Not knowing where to go or what to do. I am so naïve about all this."

"Natalie isn't. You'd manage without me, but I'm really glad to be here." He touched her shoulder and sat back. He asked Felicia to get his map out of the glove compartment. He studied it for a minute and when Natalie returned with the doughnuts and orange juice, he instructed her to take Highway 20 to Highway 101. "We'll stop in Ferndale. Stay at a little bed-and-breakfast there and let my arm heal for a day or two."

The group was quiet for a while, content to sit back and enjoy the wondrous scenery flowing past their windows. The land was mountainous with fir trees, red-berried madrone and tan -bark oak thickly covering the sides of the road. "This country is so beautiful,"

Felicia said, making an effort to relax. "I can't remember ever seeing so many different trees in one place before, and look at all the old barns on this road."

"That one looks all lacy," Lisa said.

Dylan laughed. "It's full of woodpecker holes. I'm surprised that old barn is still standing." He pointed to a road branching off to their left. "Down that road is Clear Lake's Bloody Island."

That got Mark's attention. "Bloody Island?"

Dylan nodded. "Back in the 1800's all that lived around here was mostly fur trappers and Indians. A couple of men treated the Pomo Indians cruelly and were killed in return around 1849. The soldiers retaliated and a bloody massacre followed. Over 100 Pomo men, women and children were killed and the island came to be known as Bloody Island."

"What's there now?"

"Not much of anything that I know of. A few abandoned buildings." Natalie shivered and pressed harder on the gas pedal, causing the vehicle to lurch forward.

At the same time the travelers passed by the entrance to Clear Creek, Luther paused in his observation of the prisoner room and looked up. He smiled and rose from his chair. Pushing the button that closed the curtains on his side of the one-way mirror, he called for the guard who waited outside his door. "They're close," he said. "I can feel the witch who tries to keep me from my daughter. Send out more men to find them."

Outwardly, Luther only showed his excitement with a small, tight smile. Inwardly, his insides were churning. He could feel her! The end of his mission was drawing to a close. He stepped through into his secret chamber and settled back down to watch the captive girls. Watching their fear usually had a calming effect on him and renewed his sense of power, but tonight he found himself feeling restless. He laughed sardonically. All the people in this complex were under his power. Maybe a walk around the premises would be more to his liking right now.

Luther continued to smile as people averted their eyes when he walked by. How he reveled in their submission! If only the young girl he had chosen to father his child would have been half as submissive. What a kingdom they could have run together! His brain and power mixed with her beauty. He ached to see his daughter face to face. Surely she would be excited over her destiny? Luther paused in his walk and frowned as he observed a young couple seated on the grass beside the lake. The boy was bent close to hear what the girl was saying and laughed. Luther noticed they were holding hands and the young man bent close to kiss her. Luther stood quietly behind them, his hands clasped tightly behind his back. The boy jumped when he noticed Luther standing there and the girl drew back with a shriek. Luther stared silently for several seconds before speaking. "Why aren't the two of you at prayer?"

"We…we were just headed that way," the boy stammered, nodding at the girl beside him. "Right, Patty?"

She nodded, her eyes wide with fear. Momentarily, she glanced up and met Luther's gaze. Realizing her mistake of insubordination, she quickly averted her eyes.

"Patricia Morgan. Am I correct? You have grown into quite a beauty," Luther said, reaching out to stroke her long blond hair. "I think we could find a more proper use for you." Luther motioned to his two bodyguards who stepped forward and each took one of the girl's arms.

"Oh, please," she moaned. "God…no!"

Luther bent down and with his face close to hers, growled. "I am your god, girl."

She looked over to where her friend now stood. "Robert! Help me!" The boy moved quickly to her side and tried to pull one of the guards away. Swiftly, the burly man withdrew a dagger and in one motion sliced the boy's throat and pushed him to the ground. Luther glanced over expressionlessly, his eyes cold. "Oh, the foolishness of youth! How much more pleasant it would be to just follow the simple rules I have set in place." He once again resumed his walk and allowed the guards to drag the screaming girl away.

Felicia's group was drawing close to their destination of Ferndale when they entered the stretch of highway known as the Avenue of the Giants. Redwood trees stood tall above the highway, seemingly immovable in their size and strength. The highway wound around to make room for the trees.

"I think I can stick my hand out the window and touch them as we drive by," Felicia said excitedly. "They're so close. Natalie, stop a minute. I want to get out." The group in the car watched silently as Felicia stood outside the car and looked up in awe. "Turn off the engine, please. I want to listen." Natalie obliged and the group got out to stand next to Felicia. "Listen," she told them. The wind whispered gently through the tops of the trees and a bird chirped occasionally in serenade. Felicia leaned her head back as far as she could to look way up into the leafy boughs where the sun seemed to disappear, except where it filtered through, giving the place where they stood a cathedral appearance. Moss, needles and shade-loving flowers carpeted the forest floor. Felicia sank to her knees in a pile of the soft moss.

"Do not come any closer," Felicia said softly. "Take off your sandals, for the place where you are standing is holy ground." She turned and smiled. "Exodus 3:5. This has got to be one of the most beautiful of all of God's creations." She sighed. "I wish we could stay."

Dylan had been silently watching her as she happily looked around and at her last statement he thought to himself that she was wrong. As he gazed upon the sun gently dappling her dark hair, leaves slowly raining down around her and at the lone tear working its way down her cheek, he told himself that *this* woman was God's most beautiful creation and he swore that he would give his life to protect her if it came to that.

Natalie observed the rapturous look on Dylan's face as he watched Felicia, and silently herded the children back into the car. She smiled softly. She was secure in the knowledge that what ever happened to her Felicia would be looked after. She watched sadly as Dylan knelt down beside Felicia and gently turning her face to his, kissed her.

Her only regret was that the two of them couldn't have fallen in love at a better time.

As Dylan kissed her, Felicia blushed and laid her head against his chest. "No moment could be more perfect," she whispered. Dylan agreed and hugged her tightly to him with his good arm. For several minutes they sat there, basking in the beauty around them and the stirring feelings of love. "We really should go," he told her. She nodded and walked back to the car. "We'll be married in this place," he whispered to himself before following her.

Chapter 12

Felicia slid into the back seat with the children, forcing Dylan to sit up front with her mother. She wanted to dwell on these new feelings she was experiencing without him watching her. Suddenly, she found herself feeling shy about the attention Dylan was lavishing on her. She had begun to feel comfortable in his presence until these feelings arose. Loving him would be so much easier if he shared her faith, and she was certain now that she loved him very much. The childish infatuation she had had when she was twelve was now easily turning into something much stronger.

Seated up front, Dylan was wrestling with his own emotions. He wasn't sure when his feeling of protectiveness for a friend had turned to love, but he knew that it had. Inwardly, he again cursed the man who made it necessary for them to be on the run and hiding. He wanted to woo and court Felicia in the manner she deserved. He realized that the hunt for Luther was now not only a desire for revenge for his sister's death, but to put an end to the running. He sighed and flexed his wounded arm. He would have to start working it so it would heal faster. He knew that sooner or later he would be confronting Felicia's father. Would he have to kill him? He hoped not. For the first time in a long time he regretted the possibility of taking another's life, even if he felt they deserved it. Luther was still a part of the woman he loved.

When Natalie announced that Ferndale was coming up, Felicia bolted upright, embarrassed that she had fallen asleep. Lisa, who had fallen asleep on her shoulder, groaned and sat up.

"Are we there?"

"Yes, dodo head," Mark told her. "If you wouldn't sleep all the time, you might know more of what's going on."

"Hey, Sport," Dylan spoke up. "There's nothing wrong with grabbing a nap when you can. There may come a time later when sleep will be a luxury."

"Sorry," the boy mumbled. Lisa stuck her tongue out at him and snuggled closer to Felicia.

Felicia once again took note of her surroundings. "Look at these Victorian homes. They are absolutely gorgeous!"

"Ferndale is made up mostly of weavers, painters, woodworkers and ceramists," Dylan explained. "They have made it a priority to preserve the old homes and storefronts. The locals are pretty insistent on keeping things the way they have always been. A lot of buildings had to be redone after the earthquake of 1992. Some of the homes have been made into bed-and-breakfasts and some are open for tours."

"Can we stay in one?" Lisa asked.

"If I can find one where we can also board the dogs and horses." Dylan pointed to a road going off to their right. "Turn here and I'll ask the tourist center where we can stay and restock some of our supplies." He turned to smile at Felicia. "But first, we'll spend a couple of days blending in and just being tourists."

Felicia smiled shyly back and him and nodded her thanks. As Dylan walked away from the Bronco into the tourist station, Felicia caught herself admiring his wide shoulders and lean hips and stopped herself in alarm. What was wrong with her? She had never looked at men in that way before. Never lacking in dates, Felicia enjoyed the company of young men her age, but that is how she thought of them: as boys. Dylan was a man. She admitted to herself that she enjoyed watching him and liked the way he looked to her. She sighed and sat back in her seat. She wished Honey were alive so she could talk about these new feelings. Could she talk to Natalie? She knew she was growing fond of the woman who was her mother, but didn't know if she was ready to confide personal feelings to her.

"There's a place about a mile down the road that rents out rooms and boards horses. The lady at the tourist station said she thinks they'll let us keep the dogs as long as they stay outside," Dylan told him as he slid back into the front seat.

Natalie nodded and started the engine. Within minutes they were pulling up in front of a quaint two-story Victorian house. Once again Dylan left the others in the Bronco as he approached the house. In answer to his knock, an elderly woman answered and the others watched as the two conversed for several minutes. Dylan returned and opened the back of the Bronco. "She says they have plenty of room since it's the off season and as long as the dogs don't bother the other horses boarded here, they are welcome to stay."

"Thank God," Natalie said turning off the ignition. "I am so beat."

"Can I help with the horses?" Mark asked, hurrying over to Dylan. "The girls can take care of the other stuff."

"Sure, sport," Dylan answered as their hostess approached them.

Peering into the back seat, she told them. "The kids can share one room, your wife and yourself another and the other lady can have a single room that my daughter uses when she comes to visit."

Dylan laughed. "We're not married." He looked over to where Felicia stared at him. "I'll use the single room."

The older woman nodded. "Fine. I'm Mrs. Morris and anything you need you just let me know. I live here alone now except for a young man who helps out with the horse boarding. My husband died several years ago and I'm always ready for some new company. I'll serve you breakfast and you are on your own for the other meals. If you want to prepare meals yourself, I'll allow you the use of my kitchen. I don't do this for all my guests, but as I told you earlier, it's the slow season and a lot of restaurants close early. I don't allow yelling or running in my house and I expect the kitchen to be clean when you're through. There are two bathrooms upstairs so you may want to work out using them in shifts. Any idea of how long you'll be staying?"

Dylan smiled at Natalie as the woman finished her tirade. "Just a couple of days. We really love the scenery around here and are traveling through Northern California. Just thought we'd stop and enjoy this area for a couple of days."

Mrs. Morris nodded and straightened her shoulders. "I'll show you to your rooms." She led the children upstairs to a small room with twin beds and a single closet. Natalie and Felicia were next door in a slightly larger room with one double bed, an antique armoire and a mirrored dresser stood against one wall. On the dresser sat a crystal pitcher and two glasses. Felicia glanced around her, appreciating the simplicity and the beauty of the homemade quilts smoothed across the bed. A rag rug adorned the floor beside the bed. "I'll show the gentleman to his room when he's finished with the horses. Remember; let me know if I can get you anything. Anything at all."

Natalie turned to say thank you but Mrs. Morris had already left the room. She set the suitcase down on the bed. "You don't appreciate a good bed until you've slept without one for a couple of nights, do you?"

Felicia shook her head. "I'm going outside to look around. I'll put my stuff away later, okay?"

Natalie nodded and pushed the suitcase to one side of the bed. "I'm going to take a short nap."

Felicia made her way outside to the paddock where Dylan had let the horses loose. He was nowhere around so she assumed he must have already made his way to his room. Propping one foot on the railing, she leaned her chin on her folded arms and watched aimlessly as the horses cropped at the green grass.

"Hey," Dylan said coming up behind her. He slid an arm around her waist.

"Hey," she said, pulling back.

"What's wrong?" he asked, puzzled.

She shrugged. "I'm just trying to work through some things." She gazed up at him. "I'm beginning to really care for you, Dylan and it bothers me. I always told myself I wouldn't get involved with someone who wasn't a Christian."

"I'm working on it. You can't expect me to change a lifetime of habits in a day."

She turned back to the horses, tears welling up in her eyes. "I'm scared, Dylan. So much has happened in the last few days and we don't know what tomorrow will bring. You could die, Dylan. You could die without accepting Jesus and *that* is what really scares me." She brought up one hand and furiously wiped the tears from her face. Dylan moved forward to comfort her and she stepped back again. She looked sadly at him and turned to hurry back to the house, leaving him staring after her.

Natalie awoke when Felicia entered the room and watched anxiously as Felicia flung herself down on the bed beside her. She sat up slowly. "Want to talk?"

Felicia shrugged. "I'm so confused. I think I'm falling in love with Dylan. No… That's not true. I'm already in love with him. He's not a Christian, Natalie and he's lived a very violent life. It's a part of him and I don't know how to deal with it."

Natalie placed a hand on Felicia's back. "Dylan is a good man. One of the best I've ever known." She stopped and took a deep breath. "Felicia, there's no doubting his feelings for you. He's not a man who loves easily. He's lost too many people in his life. You're not the only one grieving for Alice. She was the only family he had left. Tomorrow, it could be one of us gone. Accept his love. Trust in him as a good man and leave Dylan's salvation up to God. God can handle it. I don't think Dylan's as hard as he pretends to be." She patted her daughter's shoulder. "Dylan's parents were good Christian people and we know the type of woman Alice was. Dylan has a strong foundation. He'll come around."

Felicia rolled over and looked up at Natalie. She smiled uncertainly. "This was a mother and daughter talk, if I've ever had one."

Natalie hugged her. "That is the best thing anyone has said to me in a very long time." The two women sat quietly for several minutes until they were interrupted by Lisa barging into their room. The little girl stopped suddenly, uncertain after seeing the tears on Felicia's face. "Come here," Natalie said patting the bed beside them. "We're just having a hug session and there's always room for one more."

Felicia got up from the bed and walked back to the paddock where

Dylan still stood. He was so engrossed in his own thoughts that he didn't hear her until she was beside him. "I'm sorry, Dylan," she said quietly. "I love you." She peered up at him through the growing dusk. She stood there quietly, her uncertainty showing in every line of her body until he reached out to her.

Dylan wrapped his arms around her and drew her close to his chest. "I love you, too."

They stayed quietly together, secure in each other's company for over an hour. Night had fallen before Lisa interrupted them. "I'm hungry and Natalie is asleep again. Mark told me to find you because he's watching TV."

Felicia stooped down to the little girl's level and put an arm around her. "I'm sorry, Lisa. We lost all track of time." She smiled up at Dylan. "Let's go see what we can scrape together in Mrs. Morris's kitchen."

Dylan nodded. "I'll catch up with you in a minute."

Felicia took the little girl's hand and together they walked back to the house. Mark was seated at the table, chin in his hands. He looked up at them and scowled. "What does a body have to do to get something to eat around here?"

Felicia laughed. "Yell. Really loud."

Mark laughed and opened his mouth. Quickly, Felicia clamped her hand over his mouth. Within seconds, Dylan, Natalie and Mrs. Morris had hurried into the kitchen. Felicia and the children burst into laughter. "Sorry. Mark was hungry."

Mrs. Morris frowned and disappeared back upstairs to her room. Natalie sighed and joined the kids at the table. Dylan smiled and ruffled Mark's hair as he walked to the counter. "There's enough here for sandwiches. Guess we need to run into town tomorrow...again. Got any more of that loose cash, Natalie?"

"Yes. We're fine on money for quite a while. I've been stashing it away for a long time. Once this is all over, Felicia won't ever have to worry about money. My trust fund has been gathering interest all these years. I've rarely had need to touch it."

Dylan brought the sandwiches over to the table. With a quick glance and raised eyebrows at her mother's statement, Felicia searched the refrigerator for something to drink. "Lemonade," she announced. "Any takers?" Four hands shot up. She found some glasses and brought it all over to the table. Once Felicia was seated, Natalie held out her hands to the people on each side of her and they linked them together for prayer.

"Father, we thank you for this humble food. We thank you for keeping us safe and together for another day and we ask that you help us to trust in you in the days to follow. Amen." She squeezed Dylan's and Mark's hands before letting go. "Food tastes better with a good blessing beforehand, don't you think?" With those words, she took a large bite from her sandwich.

Dylan looked at her wonderingly before beginning to eat himself. One moment Natalie could be almost maudlin and the other totally optimistic. Her faith confused him and Felicia's open, childlike faith confused him even more. He was more comfortable relying on himself to take care of things rather than on someone, or something, he couldn't even see. He sighed inwardly. Someday, he'd take the time to research and to think it all through. Right now, there just wasn't time.

After the kids had eaten, Natalie noticed their eyes beginning to droop and ushered them upstairs to their room, leaving Dylan and Felicia to clean up. "This is nice," Felicia said.

"What?"

"This." She motioned towards the empty glasses and wadded up napkins. "It feels so ordinary. So…everyday like." She set the glasses in the sink and turning around, leaned back against the counter. "You take things for granted until it's gone."

"You'll have them all and more again."

"Maybe." She frowned. "After all this, can anything ever be ordinary again? Maybe… For you. You're used to danger and living moment to moment. I'm not. I'm twenty-one and I can't ever remember being really frightened or anxious for anything. I don't think I'll ever take life for granted again. How old are you, Dylan? Twenty-nine? Thirty?"

"More or less. Why?"

"How long have you been on your own?"

"My parents died in an accident shortly after I graduated high school. Then it was just my sister and me until last year."

"You've become pretty adept at handling things on your own, haven't you? You haven't really had to rely on others for help."

Dylan stood and went to stand in front of her. "Sweetheart, I don't know where you're headed with all these questions. What exactly is it that you want to know?"

She looked up at him, uncertainty showing on her face. "I've depended on God for everything my whole life. You have no idea what kind of peace that gives you. You struggle for everything, Dylan. I would like to see you have peace in your life."

He placed his hands on her shoulders. "Felicia. We've already had this conversation. I know how you feel and I'm aware of yours and Natalie's faith. Now is not the time. I don't want it to be that every time we are alone to talk, you bring up my lack of faith, okay?"

"Dylan…"

"Felicia…not now," he said sternly.

She nodded and turned away, busying herself with washing the dirty dishes. She turned to speak to him again, but he was gone. She hadn't heard him leave. She sighed and finished up the kitchen before heading upstairs herself.

Felicia glanced over to where Natalie lay motionless on the bed and sighed. She crossed over to the small window and looked down just in time to see Dylan crossing the yard to where the horses were corralled. She bent and leaned her elbows against the windowsill, her chin resting in her hand. She hadn't been totally honest with Dylan in the kitchen. Yes, her faith in God taking care of her was strong, but she also hadn't been more frightened of anything in her life. And she definitely wasn't feeling peaceful. When she graduated high school she had had her whole future planned. College, then a teaching job, someday a husband and kids. She hadn't planned on having an unknown mother appear and have her on the run from a deranged man who claimed he was her father. Never would she have imagined that under dire circumstances such as these would she find herself falling in love. She sighed again.

"Everything all right?" Natalie asked, sitting up in bed.

"I'm sorry. I thought you were asleep. Did I wake you?" Felicia walked over and sat on the bed.

Natalie shook her head. "No. I haven't been sleeping well for a while. I'm too afraid that I'll need to be totally awake in a second and be ready to run. Seems like I sleep with one eye open these days."

"I don't usually have trouble sleeping. It's kind of an escape, you know? Where you can go when you're depressed and can have lovely dreams. Even if I couldn't fall asleep, I'd lay there and dream of my future, or of the man I wanted to marry." She flopped back on the bed. "I'd love to know now that I even have a future to plan for."

"I know we really haven't had long to get to know each other. I also know that you can't see yourself accepting me as your mother, but I'm here for you, Felicia. Anytime you need me."

Felicia rolled over to where she was facing Natalie across the narrow space between them. "I know…and thank you. I just never thought things like what we've been going through really actually happened, outside of movies and books anyway. I never dreamed I would find myself falling in love with a man who doesn't want to know God, and being on the run for my life." She began to cry softly. "I'm very frightened." Natalie reached over and took her daughter in her arms. She never thought she would ever have the opportunity to do what so many mothers take for granted: the opportunity to love and hold the child that she bore and to give that child comfort.

"You could do worse than Dylan, even under the best circumstances. And God tells us that he doesn't give us a spirit of fear, but of hope. Remember that."

"I've grown up being taught that you don't marry outside the faith." She laughed shakily. "Not that marriage has even come up. It's kind of early for that, don't you think?" She stood up and began to pace the room, wiping the tears from her face with the sleeve of her shirt. "I tried to talk to him down in the kitchen and he got angry with me. Said now is not the time." She stopped and looked at her mother. "If now is not the time, when is? When you could die at any moment, and that's not the time?" Her voice began to rise. "What if Dylan dies tomorrow and I haven't been able to save him?"

"It's not up to *you* to save Dylan. You've done your part. Have you ever heard the saying 'Let Go and Let God'? I think now would be the perfect time to do that. You've planted the seed; now let God make it grow. Love Dylan and let God take care of the future. I really feel in my heart that Dylan will come around."

"You always seem so sure of yourself."

"Far from it, honey. I've had to take care of myself for a long time. I was younger than you are now. Right now, I'm more scared than I've ever been and I'm having to constantly remind myself of God's promises. Before, it was just me. Now it's you, Dylan and those two children."

"It seems as if I've been involved since I was born. I just didn't know it," Felicia stated bitterly. "How little control any of us really have." She shrugged. "Oh, well. I'm going to the bathroom and get ready for bed."

Natalie watched her go and shook her head sadly. Felicia could change her mood in a second, it seemed. One minute she's talking about trusting God and then in the next breath, she's talking about having no control over her life.

Natalie lay quietly in bed, listening, long after the others were quietly sleeping. She could hear the wind in the trees and the occasional hooting of an owl. How peaceful everything seemed on the surface. If she listened carefully through the open window, she thought she could hear Dylan murmuring to the horses and hear the dogs barking. While life went on in this beautiful woodland, what was Luther doing in his hideaway? Was nature as beautiful where he was, or had his evil turned even God's creation menacing? She let herself flop back against the pillow. She sent another prayer for safety heavenward. She knew that eventually they would have to face Luther and his misguided mission. Oh, how she prayed that they would be strong enough to stand against him! On the gentle breeze, she thought she could hear God's whisper reminding her that she and the others would never have to stand alone, and she finally slept.

Breakfast the next morning was silent, with Dylan and Felicia speaking very few words to each other. Natalie watched as they would look each other's way when they thought the other wasn't looking. "How about a walk around town after breakfast?" she suggested, breaking the silence. Felicia nodded and Dylan murmured in agreement.

"I was thinking that we could probably stock back up on our camping gear and food that we seem to always be leaving behind," Dylan said, smiling. *And give us something to do besides sit and stare at each other*, he added to himself.

The group made the Ferndale Chamber of Commerce their first stop and picked up a tourist map of the town and surrounding area. They fit in their shopping between tours of restored Victorian homes and a local museum. Felicia kept Lisa close by her side and Mark followed on Dylan's heels, enabling the two adults to not have to speak much to each other. Several times throughout the day, Felicia would think of something to say to Dylan, but would feel uncomfortable about her behavior the night before and would choose to remain silent. Dylan would also start to say something, but Felicia's standoffishness would stop him. Natalie watched the two of them and wished fervently for a way to help them. She prayed several times for God to bridge the rift between the two.

As dusk began to settle upon the town, the group headed back to the bed-and-breakfast. Once there, Dylan stored their purchases in the car and unfolded the map from the glove compartment, while the women carried in the food. Felicia grabbed a couple of apples from one of the bags and headed out to the paddock. Dylan looked up from his map and watched as Felicia walked away. He turned back to the map and found he couldn't concentrate. Her face swam across the paper before him. He turned and leaned back against the hood of the truck and watched her as the first horse ambled over, curious about what she was holding out to him. The light from the kitchen spilled out across the lawn and Felicia stood out clearly against the shadows behind her. She reached up and scratched behind the horse's ear while he ate the apple. Dylan stood silently for several minutes, watching her before he allowed himself to follow her.

Unsure of his reception, Dylan softly touched her shoulder. Felicia turned around quickly, without speaking and pulled his head close to hers for a kiss. Dylan smiled and embraced her. "I'm sorry."

Laying her forehead against his chest, she shook her head. "No. I'm sorry. I should never have tried to force you into making a decision that you're not ready to make." She tilted her head back and peered through the deepening dusk. "What now?"

"We take it one day at a time. I spoke with Mrs. Morris this morning about purchasing a horse. She isn't selling one of her own but said there was a man just a couple of miles down the road that would possibly sell us one. There's just too many of us for the two horses. My arm is beginning to heal nicely and I think it's time we started to really think about where Luther is. I think we may be heading in the wrong direction."

"Where do we look?"

He shrugged. "I'm going to call a buddy of mine tomorrow. It's risky and probably a long shot, but I'm hoping that he can maybe dig something up for us. Maybe let us know where Luther's people are spotted the most often. I'd like to only stay here a day or two."

"Lisa and Mark are so young. Couldn't we just leave them here with Mrs. Morris?"

"Luther knows by now that we have them. I don't think he'll let them alone now. At least if they're with us, we can do our best to protect them. I'll think about it."

Felicia turned and, keeping Dylan's arms around her waist, leaned back against him. The two dogs ran up and lay at their feet. Content in each other's company, they watched the horses graze until it was too dark to see. Dylan then took Felicia's hand and led her to the front porch where they sat in a porch swing. Natalie observed them from the window where she was helping Mrs. Morris with the dishes, and smiled.

Chapter 13

Felicia stretched and pulled the blankets back up around her neck. The morning breeze coming through the open bedroom window was chilly and she burrowed deeper into the blankets. She could hear faint murmuring from the kitchen downstairs and recognized Dylan's voice, along with her mother's. She savored the memories of the closeness she had shared with Dylan the night before and smiled. Through the open window she could hear the occasional barking of the dogs and a whinny from one of the horses. Soon the laughter of the two children joined in the morning sounds and Felicia forced herself to get up from the bed. She hurriedly pulled on a pair of jeans under the oversized tee shirt she had worn to bed and joined the others in the kitchen.

Natalie and Dylan were enjoying the morning over cups of hot coffee when Felicia entered. "Good morning," she greeted them.

"Good morning," Natalie said back. "Did you sleep well? Want a cup of coffee?"

"Yes to both."

"You decided to sleep in this morning, didn't you?" Dylan teased.

She smiled lazily back. "Yes, and it felt wonderful. I couldn't help myself. I just lay there and listened to the sounds of the morning and snuggled down under my blankets. It was heavenly."

"What did you listen to?"

"Oh, you. Natalie. The kids. The animals."

"Dylan," Natalie called from where she stood by the window. "Come here! Quickly!"

Dylan jumped up and hurried over to join her at the window. A strange man stood outside talking to Mark and Lisa while they were at the horse paddock. He leaned nonchalantly against the railing, talking to the children and occasionally glancing towards the house. Mark was sitting astride the top railing and Lisa was leaning through. Suddenly, without warning, the man grabbed Mark around the waist and stood him on the ground. Without letting go of Mark, he reached for Lisa's hand and tried to pull them with him. Natalie gasped in alarm and rushed toward the door. Dylan reached out a hand to stop her, shaking his head. "Mark!" Dylan yelled through the window. "Get your sister and come eat!"

Mark jerked his hand free and grabbing his sister, took off at a run for the house. The stranger stood watching them, a smile on his face. Mark stopped at the door and glanced back. The man waved and, Dstill smiling, turned and slowly walked into the woods behind the house.

Natalie yanked the door open and pulled the children inside. "Who was that man?" she demanded. "What did he want?" She grabbed Mark by the shoulders and shook him. "Tell me!" Tears welled up in her eyes and rolled down her face. Realizing that she was shouting, she stopped and put her hands to her face. She kneeled before the children and looked up into their startled faces. "I'm sorry. I shouldn't be yelling at you like that. You really scared me. I thought we had lost the two of you."

"Calm down, Natalie," Dylan told her. "Mark? Do you know that man?"

He shook his head. "We were petting the horses and all of a sudden there he was. Right behind us. He said he was a friend of my dad's. I didn't believe him, but he just kept talking. He knew our names and our parents' names. I wasn't really scared until he tried to grab me."

Lisa had her arm around Natalie's neck and was crying softly. "He said he was going to take us to see our mom and dad."

"Mom and Dad are dead!" Mark yelled at her. "Accept it!"

"Hey, sport," Dylan cautioned. "There's no need for that. Yelling at your sister doesn't solve anything." Dylan led him over to the table. "Come sit down and we'll get you a bowl of warm oatmeal." He nodded over the boy's head at Felicia for her to get their breakfast. "Now, Mark. I've got to ask you a question and I need a truthful answer. Take a minute to think about it." Mark nodded. "Where are the dogs? Did you see them this morning?"

"I heard them earlier," Felicia spoke up. "But that was before I got out of bed."

Dylan transferred his attention to her. "Where did you hear them? What direction?"

"Out behind the paddock…I think."

"Mark?"

"I didn't see them, Dylan. They were gone when Lisa and I went outside."

Dylan sprinted up the stairs to his room and grabbed his pistol. Coming back through the kitchen he ordered the women to lock the door behind him. "I'm going out to look for them. That man would never have gotten that close to the kids if the dogs had been around. Give me a half hour. If I'm not back, pack up the kids and leave. Don't wait for me."

"Go where?" Felicia followed him. "Dylan?"

"Lock the door!"

Felicia turned to Natalie. "Why? Things were so great last night and earlier this morning. How do these people keep finding us?"

Natalie shook her head in bewilderment. "I don't know. He always seems to know where I am." She finished spooning the oatmeal into bowls for the kids. "Let's feed these two. I have a feeling we'll be moving on again today." With another glance in the direction Dylan had gone, Felicia closed the door and engaged the lock before joining the others at the table.

Dylan dashed off in the direction Felicia had said she had heard the dogs. Hurrying, yet afraid of what he might find, Dylan's heart beat fiercely in his chest. The trees behind the paddock closed in tightly around him, letting in very little of the morning sun. He stood still, trying to slow his breathing and listen. He kept his gun ready. For several seconds he heard nothing but the chirping of the birds. Then he heard it. A faint whimpering, off to his left. With his gun in his right hand, he sprinted off. Several yards deeper into the underbrush, he found his dogs.

Duke was lying next to the body of his companion, softly whimpering as he licked the fatal wound across the other dog's throat. Luke's neck had been slashed from one ear to the other and there was a stab wound in his right shoulder. The dog's blood soaked the ground beneath him. Dylan's breath caught in a sob as he slowly knelt beside the dog. Duke nudged his arm and whimpered. "Oh, Luke!" Dylan said, a sob catching in his throat. Tenderly, he lifted the body of his faithful friend and motioning for Duke to follow, he walked dejectedly back towards the boarding house.

As he entered the yard of the house, a bullet whined past his year. Dylan dropped the dog, fell to one knee and drew his pistol. He scanned the woods behind him and dove for cover as another shot rang out.

"Dylan!" Felicia screamed from the house.

He waved for her to stay in and scrambled back into the woods. He stayed low and kept his breathing shallow. He strained his ears to hear anything out of the ordinary. He was shocked and fell over as Duke barreled past him, barking ferociously. "Duke! Stay!" he ordered. The dog came back reluctantly. Dylan held the dog's collar and listened. There! The snapping of a twig sounded abnormally loud in the stillness. He jumped to his feet and sprinted through the brush in the direction of the sound he had heard. Duke stayed close to him, resuming his barking.

Dylan ran deep into the forest, past the place where he had located his dog and stopped. He remained motionless for several minutes. There were no other gunshots or sounds other than the birds. He stuck his pistol back into the waistband of his jeans, slapped his leg for the dog to follow and loped back to where he had dropped Luke.

"He's coming back," Lisa told them from her perch on the kitchen counter, "and he's carrying one of the dogs."

"Oh, no," Felicia whispered. "Oh, Dylan." Tears coursed down her cheeks. "Which one?"

"Luke." Dylan lay him on the ground next to the steps. Duke sat close by, his forehead creased in confusion. "They *killed* my dog. My dog!" Dylan cursed and hung his head. He wiped his hand roughly across his face to wipe away the tears. Then he stood up, his face marred with anger. "I've got to bury him. Pack up. We're leaving when I'm finished."

"Who was shooting at you? Did you find them?" Natalie had withdrawn her own pistol when the shooting started.

"No. He was gone." He disappeared around the corner of the house and returned shortly, carrying a shovel. He avoided the concerned eyes of the two women and handing the shovel to Mark, once again picked up Luke's body. He headed off in the direction of the paddock, leaving the boy to follow.

Natalie walked up behind Felicia and put an arm around her shoulder. Gently, she drew her back to the house. "Come on. Dylan will be wanting to leave, once he's buried Luke." Felicia nodded and wiped away her own tears.

Mechanically, Lisa returned to eating, her oatmeal now cold, while the two women got together the few things that they had unpacked the day before. When Felicia headed upstairs, Natalie sagged wearily against the counter. The strain was wearing on her. Daily, she felt her resolve weakening and considered once again whether she should leave and head out on her own. Try to lead Luther away from Felicia and the others. She prayed again to God for strength.

Dylan came back by the time they were finished and tossed backpacks and saddles bags on the kitchen table. "Repack," he told them. "Only what will fit in these. We're leaving the car in exchange for Mrs. Morris's two horses. Leave her a note would you, Natalie?" Without waiting for an answer, he disappeared outside again.

Natalie and Felicia looked at each other and began to sort out what was important enough to take. Felicia sighed. *Warm things,* she thought to herself: *coats, pants, and long sleeved shirts.* She leaned back on her knees over the open suitcase. She shrugged and getting up, went over to Natalie. "The blankets are in the Bronco. You have the guns and ammunition. I've put warm clothes and a coat in each back pack." She shook her head. "I don't know how to pack a saddle bag or roll a blanket to tie on the back of a horse! I barely even know *how* to ride a horse!" Her voice began to rise. "I have absolutely no idea of what to pack!"

"There are matches over the stove, I think. We'll take what we need from Mrs. Morris and I'll leave her money. It'll be fine. Run out to the car, Lisa and get the blankets. I'll roll them. Felicia, you stuff non-perishable food items in these saddlebags." Natalie began assigning duties to the other two. "Felicia, go and see if you can find some rope...or twine. I've already packed the medicine chest and we bought canteens yesterday. It'll have to do." She stood back and scratched her head, contemplating the pile that lay before her.

Dylan came back in and saw that a couple of the backpacks had hardly anything in them. "Everyone wears a backpack. Even the kids."

Felicia spoke up. "Where are we going, Dylan?"

"The mountains. We've got to try and find a place he can't get to us until I'm healed enough to fight. The run through the woods and carrying Luke has my arm throbbing. Obviously, towns are a bad idea."

"I saw a movie once," Lisa said, her mouth full of cereal. "Where these people were running from the bad guys and the bad guys kept finding them. One of the good guys had a thingy inside of him that let the bad guys know where he was."

"That's dumb," Mark told her. "That's the movies."

Natalie looked up quickly from her work and glanced worriedly over at Dylan. He was staring at Lisa and Natalie rapidly lowered her head again. Could it be? She shook her head. She'd know, wouldn't she? Natalie squared her shoulders and zipped up the last bag she was working on.

"I think I'm finished," Felicia announced.

Dylan stood in the doorway. "Well...that's that I guess. Mark, you ride on my horse, Lisa you're with Felicia and Natalie, you're on your own. The fourth horse will carry the supplies that won't fit on the horses we're riding. I figure we'll head north into the Shasta

National Forest and try to prepare ourselves for a confrontation. We can't run forever." He looked around the group. "Everyone ready?"

They looked around at each other. Each person was trying to push down their own fear in order to help the others. Even the children seemed to realize that they would have to be strong for the sake of the group.

"Dylan," Natalie interrupted quietly. "Don't you think that Luther is probably south of here? Maybe around Bloody Island? That seems to be the most likely spot. The island is uninhabited, except for a few empty buildings. There are forests around that part of the state that are thick enough for him to have a group of followers living in, away from prying eyes."

Dylan shook his head. "I agree, Natalie. But right now, I'm in no condition to fight one of his friends. Shasta is much closer and we can lose ourselves in there. It'll be rough, but I think we can do it and it'll be much harder for someone to follow us if we're on horseback. We can go in deep, far away from the roads."

Chapter 14

Dylan hastily scribbled a note for Mrs. Morris, leaving his Bronco in trade for the horses, telling her he'd be back to trade the horses back to her at another time. Natalie lay some money on the table and walked out. He looked out the door to where the others were waiting. To anyone who might be watching, it looked exactly as it was. Like they were running again. He looked up at the overcast sky. The nights were already cold and the days were getting colder. It bothered him that they would be in the mountains during the winter. The responsibility for the two women and children rested heavily on his shoulders. From somewhere buried deep within himself, he recalled a bible verse he had learned as a child about coming all who were weary and heavy burdened. He couldn't remember the rest. He noticed that Natalie and Felicia appeared to be praying. *Well, good,* he thought to himself. It couldn't hurt and they needed all the help they could get. He walked out to the others and still, without speaking, checked his rifle tied to the back of his horse and then checked his supply of bullets. He shrugged and swung up on to the horse, motioning for the others to do the same. He held his hand out to pull Mark up behind him and set off into the woods behind the house, the others following.

A pair of eyes watched silently from the other side of the clearing. The man hidden there smiled, and turning, walked to where a truck was waiting on an old logging road. He picked up the cellular phone on the seat of the truck and began talking.

"They're all there?" the voice on the other end asked.

"Yes, sir. Everyone. Kids, too."

"Keep on their trail and don't let yourself be seen. Bring me the young woman and the children. Kill the witch, and the man if you have to. They are of no use to me."

"They've taken off on horseback, sir."

"Do I have to do your thinking for you also? Get a horse." The phone clicked and the man in the truck put the phone back into its receiver. He saw there were still a couple of horses in the paddock. He grabbed the cell phone and a satchel from the passenger seat and sprinted in the direction of the house. He had very little supplies in the satchel he carried and knew that Luther would not be lenient enough for him to stop into town before following his orders. He cursed when he saw that Dylan had locked the door behind him. Picking up a small planter, he tossed it through the window and hurriedly climbed inside, scouring the kitchen for food and something to cover himself with at night. He cursed again as he grabbed the plastic tablecloth off the table, scattering the money Natalie had left, and then ran for the paddock.

Natalie rode at the rear of the group and glanced behind her repeatedly. She rode with her pistol tucked into the waistband of her jeans and fidgeted with it, trying to get it to sit more comfortably. Lisa's innocent remark about a tracking device kept nagging at her mind. She had had the tattoo removed that had branded her as one of Luther's followers. Was it possible that he had also planted a tracking device? Something he had inserted under the skin? The thought that she might be leading him right to their little group made her blood run cold. Something within herself told her that traveling north wasn't going to prolong anything. Luther was on a mission and would stop at nothing until he had obtained that which he had sat out to get. The Luther she knew would choose a place to live that had a past history of violence and bloodshed. She sighed. Maybe Dylan was right and this would help them be better prepared.

"I have to go to the bathroom," Lisa said quietly from behind Felicia.

"Can't you wait a little while? We just started out an hour ago."

"No. I really have to go." Felicia could feel the girl shifting her weight.

"All right." She spurred the horse a little quicker until she was riding alongside Dylan. "Lisa has to use the restroom."

Dylan looked over at the little girl. Lisa gave him a small smile. "Jeez," he muttered under his breath. He pulled the horses off the trail they had been following and rode a little further into the trees. "Make it quick," he told her. "Mark, you might as well go too." The kids slid down and disappeared behind some bushes. Dylan uncapped one of the canteens and passed it around. "We're being followed," he told the women quietly.

"How do you know?" Felicia asked looking behind them. "I haven't seen or heard anyone."

He motioned toward the dog. "Look at Duke." The dog was staring down the trail in the direction they had come from. His ears were standing straight up on his head and the hair along his neck bristled. Duke growled softly.

"Won't he bark and give us away?" Natalie asked alarmed. "Shouldn't we get the kids?"

Dylan shook his head. "I've already motioned for him to be silent. Let the kids finish their business. I'm just going to circle around and surprise our visitor. Watch the kids and keep them quiet." Dylan motioned for Duke to follow him and set off quietly in the direction they had come.

He placed each foot carefully in order to remain silent and held his gun ready before him. He squatted down behind a low bush and watched as the man rode slowly past where he was hiding. When the man pulled abreast of him, Dylan rose and walked out to stand in the trail directly in front of the horse. The horse reared, knocking the man to the ground. Dylan stepped quickly over to the fallen man and held his gun steadily at the man's chest.

"Ok, buddy," he said. "Mind telling me why you're following us?"

"I'm not following anyone. This is a public trail. I'm just out riding." The man's eyes widened as Dylan cocked the gun.

"Really? Without a saddle?"

"Yeah! I happen to prefer riding that way!"

Dylan planted his boot in the middle of the man's chest and shoved him back. "I'm having a little trouble believing you. Why did you try to grab those two children?"

"I don't know what you're talking about!" The man's face reddened as Dylan's boot moved upwards and planted itself on his neck.

"Two questions, pal. Where's Luther's camp and how many more of you are following us?"

"Luther who?" the man sneered. He choked as Dylan stepped down harder on his neck.

"Give him a message for me, will you? Tell him that I will find him and I will kill him."

"He'll find you first. You have no power against a master such as he!"

Dylan smiled and swung the gun hard against the man's head, knocking him unconscious. He walked over and took the reins of the horse. He pointed the horse in the right direction and slapping its withers, sent it home. "Come on, Duke. I think we've left enough of a message."

The children rejoined Natalie and Felicia and the two women had them climb back on their horses to wait until Dylan returned. They wanted to be able to leave quickly if they sensed danger.

"What's taking him so long?" Felicia asked nervously. "What if something's gone wrong?"

"Nothing's gone wrong," Natalie reassured her. "Dylan's all right."

They jumped as they heard noise in the underbrush coming their way. Felicia quickly mounted her horse while Natalie withdrew her gun from the waistband of her jeans and aimed it in the direction the noise had come from. They relaxed visibly when Dylan emerged.

"Not going to shoot me, are you?" he asked smiling. "Save your bullets for another day."

"Did you kill him, Dylan?" Mark asked as he climbed down in order for Dylan to mount the horse.

"No," Dylan answered wearily. "I didn't kill him. Just gave him a little message." With a left pull on the reins, Dylan guided the horse back to the trail, then crossed it and led them into the trees on the other side. Natalie moved her horse alongside his.

"You the same as killed that man. Luther doesn't tolerate failure. Of *any* kind."

Dylan shrugged. "Not our problem, is it? Would you rather I did kill him? Put a bullet in his head?"

She shook her head. "No. Killing the messenger isn't the right idea. I just want to let you know what kind of man Luther really is."

"I *know* what kind of man he is! You don't have to feel as if you need to warn me every time we run into one of his errand boys."

"I'm sorry. I forget sometimes that you're as involved in all this as we are."

Dylan shrugged her off. "What about Mark and Lisa? We need to find a safe place for them. I thought at first they'd be safer with us. That maybe Luther would still go after them if they were somewhere else. Now, I'm thinking that maybe he'll focus *only* on Felicia and let the kids be. It'll be tougher to fight him with the kids along. What do you think?"

"You're not leaving us anywhere!" Mark shouted angrily from behind him. "We'll just run away again. I can help you. I know I can!"

"He won't hurt them," Natalie told him. "They're easy converts. Luther takes in children all the time. I really don't know of anyone we can leave them with. I haven't made many friends over the years. What about you?"

He shook his head. "Too many questions would be asked. There use to be a lady I knew once. She lived over in Weaverville. She was a friend of my mother's. She might be willing to keep the kids for a couple of days. We're headed in that direction anyway. It won't hurt to check."

"Do you trust her?"

"As much as I trust anyone."

"I won't go, I tell you!" Dylan reached back to hold on to Mark who was trying to slide off the horse. Natalie reached over to help while Felicia rode up closer to see what the commotion was about. "Lisa! They want to send us away! Get down! Run!" Lisa sat silently behind Felicia, uncomprehending what Mark was so upset about.

"Hey, sport," Dylan said, trying to restore peace. "We'll reconsider. There's time. Okay?"

Mark nodded sullenly and settled down. The group was quiet again as they rode. The temperature began to drop as night fell and Dylan began searching for a place to spend the night. He was hoping for an abandoned cabin or barn. They were going to be spending enough nights on the cold ground. The forest was thickening and they had left the trail behind hours ago. He glanced over his shoulder to see how the others were faring. Felicia rode silently, her head down. Dylan sighed again as he observed the weariness on the children's faces and the slump of their shoulders. Natalie showed the least sign of fatigue as she cast her eyes continually around them. *How did Luther's men keep finding them*, he wondered. He had a feeling that Natalie knew more than she was telling. Did she really know where Luther's camp was? Did he have any weaknesses that would help them?

He heard sounds of traffic close by and urged his horse to pick up the pace. The foliage was thick and as he rode out onto the road he was startled by the blaring of a horn. He jerked roughly on the reins, causing his horn to rear as he narrowly escaped being struck by the car roaring by. Mark yelped as his grip on Dylan's waist broke and he slid to the ground. Dylan shook his head in anger. How could he not have seen it? He heard the car and walked the horse out in front of it like he had no brain in his head! He struggled to calm his horse and slid quickly to the ground before he rushed over to see if Mark was hurt. The boy was standing, rubbing his backside.

"You okay? Not hurt, are you?

Mark shook his head. "I'm okay. I wasn't paying attention. I was almost asleep I think."

Dylan looked around him and grabbed the reins to the packhorse, which had started to wander off. The road was clear in both directions. It didn't seem to be a well-traveled road so he motioned for the others to follow him across. With his luck he had probably happened to find the only vehicle in miles.

Felicia had listened to the exchange between her mother and Dylan regarding the man they had left in the woods behind them. She agreed with Dylan that the children should be left somewhere for their safety. But how safe would they really be? Luther's reach seemed to be very long. What if he took the children anyway? What if he used them as bait? Then they would be hunting Luther on his terms. She shook her head wearily. It was all so frightening and unreal to her. She had lived her past twenty-one years feeling safe and loved. Nothing could have prepared her for this. Her heart cried out to God to save them. She believed in man's free will, but where was hers and the children's will in all this? None of them had asked for, or done anything to warrant all this. Were they all paying for a mistake that Natalie had made as a youth? She hung her head as a tear coursed down her cheek. She really needed to toughen up and stop crying. It seemed that was all she did anymore. The children didn't need to see her cry. They were trying to be strong through all this. They were only children, after all.

She felt Lisa's head fall forward to rest against her back. She smiled softly. The little girl appeared to have fallen asleep. She slowly reached up and wiped away the tear. Squaring her shoulders, she fixed her gaze ahead and gasped. She emerged through the trees as the horn blared and Dylan's horse reared, causing Mark to fall. Lisa woke with a scream and Felicia shushed her as she watched Dylan helped Mark back up on the horse and lead them all across the road.

A mile or two further and they emerged from the woods back onto the same road as it had wound around. Ahead of them was a small store with a sign that read 'Hank's Grocery.' The store was built of weathered, grey planking, with a small porch that ran the length of the front of the store. On the porch steps sat an elderly man, dressed in overalls and a flannel shirt, chewing tobacco and calmly whittling a piece of wood.

"Want to stop here to grab something to eat?" Dylan asked the others. "Save the provisions for when we really need them?" Natalie nodded, and Dylan led them up to the store.

The old man looked up as they dismounted. "Evening."

"Good evening," Dylan replied. "Are you open?"

"Always open." The man spit a stream of tobacco towards their feet, "'cept for night time. I close after dark. It's about dark now. You folks not from around here."

"No, sir. We're camping. We're taking the horses so we can get to the really good places." Dylan looked at the rest of the group and silently motioned for them to let him do the talking. "Just stopped by to get some food, maybe some ammunition if you have it. I'd like to squeeze in some hunting."

"Well... I've got a small variety of food. Ammo too." He looked over at the others. "This your family you got with ya?"

"My wife, kids and mother-in-law."

The man spat again. "That so? You look kinda young for kids of that age."

Felicia and Natalie glanced worriedly at each other. Dylan frowned, clearly tiring of the questioning. "We're older than we look. Do you always interrogate your customers this way?"

"Nope. Just being neighborly." The man stood. "Name's Hank. Come on in. We'll do business." He led the way into his store. Dylan whispered for the others to stay outside.

It took a few moments for his eyes to adjust to the gloom of the store. Although dusty, the store appeared to be well organized and Dylan quickly found the items he was looking for. He picked up several boxes of the type of ammunition that he and Natalie used and grabbed a loaf of bread, some lunchmeat, apples. Smiling to himself, he grabbed a few bottles of soda. He plopped his purchases on the counter. "Do you happen to have a map of the area north of here?"

The storekeeper glanced up quickly. "Hunting up Shasta way?"

"No, sir. Just passing through there." Dylan handed the man his money and grabbing the bags, exited the store.

"We're not eating here," he told the others. "We'll ride on a little ways and then stop. This guy is too nosey."

"Do you think he's one of Luther's men?" Natalie asked.

"No. But he talks too much. If they figure out we stopped here and they come by, I think he'll give out way too much information"

Chapter 15

Michael stood stiffly and silently before the cold, staring man sitting behind the desk. The only sign of nervousness Michael showed was the sweat beaded upon his brow. He had stood this way for several minutes already, while the other man silently scrutinized him. Michael's parents had already turned their backs to him when he entered the camp only a few minutes earlier.

Luther leaned back in his chair, enjoying the silent anxiousness of the young man standing before his desk. Purposely, Luther had not spoken since uttering the command to enter. To his credit, Michael had come straight to Luther's office upon entering the camp.

"I am very disappointed in you," Luther stated, his cold words slicing through Michael. "Failure on the part of any of my subjects tastes very bitter to me. Are you aware of the penalty of failure, Michael?"

Michael swallowed hard and continued to look straight ahead. "Death, sir."

Luther rubbed his chin. "You're correct. But... you have long been a favorite of mine. Almost like the son I never had." Luther rose from his desk and walked to stand before Michael. "I am willing to give you another chance." He folded his hands behind his back and began pacing. "I am sending..." He was interrupted by a knock on his office door. "Enter."

The man, whom Dylan had sent back as messenger, timidly approached. "Sir! A message, sir!"

"Proceed."

The man took a deep breath. "I followed the woman and her

group north of Ferndale where I was attacked by the man who travels with them. He knocked me from my horse and sent me back to you with a message."

"What was the order I had given you?"

"To bring the girl back to you, sir."

"And exactly how did you attempt to accomplish this task?" Luther's pale eyes bore into the man's.

"I attempted to kidnap the young boy, sir. I had thought to use him as bait."

"A futile attempt I gather, since you have returned without *any* of them."

The man's shoulder's slumped imperceptibly. "Yes, sir."

"And the message you have deigned to bring back to me?"

"The man said to tell you that he would kill you, sir."

"Really?" Luther walked back behind his desk and opened a drawer. "A difficult task for a mere mortal man. This man's ambitions must run very high." Luther withdrew a small pistol from the drawer and matter-of-factly shot the man through the center of his forehead. He then refocused his attention to Michael, who had by this time begun to sweat rather profusely.

"Now, then. As I was saying, I was already aware that this imbecile had failed. I am sending you to kill the witch, who has taken my daughter. Feel free to dispose of her and the man in any way you desire. Bring my daughter and the two children back to me." He walked back to stand very closely to Michael. "Take any others who may be of help to you. Do not fail me again, Michael. And dispose of this body before you go, would you?"

Michael swallowed. "Yes, sir." He bent and grabbing the dead man's ankles, dragged him from the room. He dumped the dead man on the ground outside of the building where Luther's office was and strode angrily to his own room on the campus. He flung around the meager belongings he kept there, muttering to himself. "My whole life! I've spent my whole life following that woman around, and for what?

No, 'Thank you, Michael'

No, 'Job well done. Michael'

Well, I'll show him! I'll bring her in and kill the witch myself!" He grabbed a duffel bag from beneath the bed and stalked from his room.

Luther stroked his chin as he watched Michael's tantrum from a hidden camera. He made sure that all his people were watched by someone. He turned to the man standing impassively behind him. "Get someone to follow him. I think Michael may have too much of a personal interest in this. The young fool thinks he's going out alone." The man nodded and silently left the room.

It didn't take Michael long to gather up his few belongings and after having done this, he went in search of his parents. He found them standing alone by the shore of the lake. "I've been sent to bring Felicia back. You'll both regret shunning me when I'm through. I will succeed at this and then you will be dead to me too." He turned and ran to one of the small boats. He tossed his bag roughly into the bottom of it and sped to the opposite bank. His mind spun in circles during the short ride over. To be shunned by Felicia was bad enough, but to be shunned by his parents was a personal slap in the face. It was all Natalie's fault. If she hadn't of come into the picture, Michael would have succeeded. He swore to himself that he would witness her death firsthand.

Chapter 16

Clouds were building by the time the group stopped to eat their lunch so Dylan rushed them through their sandwiches and drinks, keeping a wary eye on the weather. Even then, the winds had picked up by the time they were finished.

"Looks bad," Natalie told him.

Dylan nodded. "We've got to find a place to wait it out. It's getting too cold for us to be getting soaked." He pulled out the map he had brought. "Only thing is, I don't know anyone around here. The woman I was counting on is still several miles farther north." Lightening cracked over their heads and Lisa ducked, screaming. "We've got to find somewhere to shelter…now. It's too open here." He jammed the map back into his backpack. "Follow me."

By the time they had found a shelter, they were all soaked to the skin. The shelter Dylan had found for them was nothing more than a hollowed out space in the side of a hill. It offered some shelter from the rain and blocked most of the wind. The women and children jumped quickly from their horses and hurried into the small cave while Dylan tethered the horses to a tree. The women quickly set about stripping the children's wet clothes from them and Dylan began foraging around in the dark overhang for dry wood. Soon, he had coaxed a small fire and they all sat huddled and shivering around it.

Dylan glanced silently around him at the pale faces illuminated by the fire's glow. Natalie sat with her arms around the two children, trying to share her body heat with them. Mark sat up straight, his feet stretched out in front of him toward the fire's warmth, his eyes fixed unblinking on the flames. Lisa huddled close to Natalie's side, sharing a blanket and shivering, her eyes closed. The little girl flinched each time lightning cracked or the thunder rolled. Dylan looked over at Felicia, who sat staring into the fire, knees bent, her arms wrapped around them. She caught him staring and smiled wanly before turning back to the fire. Again, Dylan was hit strongly by the overwhelming task he had undertaken by trying to protect this group. How could he do it alone? Natalie seemed strong and determined and Felicia had her moments of weakness, but her inner strength always seemed to overcome the weakness. The children tried to be brave, but with each encounter of one of Luther's followers, he could see their courage fading. He had to find a place to leave them. They could not all go on running indefinitely.

Natalie rose from her place by the fire and began to unroll the bedrolls. Felicia saw her working and got up to fix more sandwiches. She smiled over at the dog that watched her as she prepared their dinner. She tossed him a slice of ham and laughed as he caught it mid-air, tail wagging for more.

"I've got a can of food in my pack for him," Dylan offered. "I'll feed him. Save the food for us."

"Okay." Felicia smiled impishly and tossed the dog another slice of the ham after Dylan had turned away. Once they had all eaten and the children were lying tucked into their sleeping bags, Felicia and Natalie rejoined Dylan by the fire.

"Well," Felicia began. "You must have some sort of plan. I can't imagine that you plan on having the five of us wander endlessly through these woods."

"You're right. My plan right now is to get these kids north to my friend and hope they'll be safe there. I'm thinking that if they're not with us, maybe Luther will let them be and focus his concentration on us." He tossed the map to Natalie. "I'm also thinking that after that we'll head back south, but you know Luther better than the rest of us and Northern California covers a lot of miles. See if you can't make a guess. Study the map and see if you still believe he may be around Bloody Island." They sat quietly while Natalie studied the map.

She studied the names of every mountain, National Forest and lake listed. On the back of the map was written a little local history and she read that as well. While she read and studied the map, she prayed for guidance. Her time spent with Luther had been short and was such a long time ago. For her to be able to help Dylan, God would have to help *her*. There! Clear Lake! She should have known sooner. Clear Lake was thought to be the oldest lake in North America and was California's largest lake. Nestled at the foot of Mt. Konocti, an active volcano, it was surrounded by 100 miles of shoreline. Although it was visited each year by many tourists for its hot mineral springs, there was enough land for a small gathering of people to hide effectively. At the northern end of the lake was an island dubbed "Bloody Island" by locals. She read of the Indian massacre there and knew that that sort of history would appeal to Luther. If he wasn't on the island itself, she felt he would be somewhere in the surrounding area. "Here," she said handing the map back to Dylan. "This place would appeal to him. I still think he might be around there."

Dylan nodded. "I've been there. A pretty busy place for his activities, but I see the possibilities." He didn't add that local disappearances in that area had risen in the last few months. He traced his finger from where they were now to where they believed Luther to be. "We've got to head back the way we came. We'll travel through the Mendocino National Forest and avoid roads as much as possible. It's quite a ways from here. On horseback at least, but we'll be able to travel faster once we drop the kids off."

"What if your friend isn't there?" Felicia asked, glancing over to where the children were sleeping.

"She's never gone for long. We might have to wait a day or two. Give us a chance to figure things through. But, it'll be cold there. Most likely they've gotten several inches of snow by now."

"It's getting cold enough here. I don't think we're prepared for snow."

Dylan agreed. "I've got to get to town to buy snow suits. The rain has stopped. I'll go now. I should be back by morning. Midday at the latest." Duke sat up. "Stay boy. Watch the others."

131

"Wait, Dylan," Natalie held out her hand to stop him. "There's something I need to tell you." She took a deep breath as Dylan watched her expectantly. "I think Lisa may have been right about a tracking device," she told him quietly.

"What?"

She pulled down the collar of her shirt to reveal the scar where she had had the tattoo removed. "What if it's true? What if the device is under the skin where the tattoo was? There has always been a pebble size bump there. I just thought maybe it was scar tissue."

Dylan squatted down and peered at the scar, running his finger softly over the spot. "What do you want me to do?"

"Cut it out."

"Cut it out!" Felicia exclaimed.

"Natalie? Are you sure?" Dylan asked.

"Yes. There is a filet knife in my pack that should be sharp enough. Felicia, get the first aid kit." Felicia hurried to rummage through Natalie's pack and went to hand the knife to Dylan.

"Use the alcohol to clean around her scar," he told Felicia as he went to hold the knife in the flames of the fire. He squatted down next to Natalie again and peered into her eyes. "This is going to hurt, Natalie. I don't have anything to give you for the pain, besides a few aspirin."

She nodded and closed her eyes. "It shouldn't have to be deep."

"Hold my hand," Felicia told her as she took Natalie's hand in hers.

Natalie gripped her daughter's hand tightly and gasped as Dylan broke the skin of her shoulder. He made a small incision about an inch in width and puckered the skin together to apply pressure around the wound. Natalie whimpered softly. Dylan pressed harder and soon held in his fingers what resembled a small watch battery. He crushed it between two rocks and tossed it into the fire. Natalie took several deep breaths as Felicia cleaned and bandaged the wound.

"You okay?" Dylan asked.

Natalie nodded. "Wish I would've thought of it sooner."

"You are a remarkably strong woman, Natalie. But did you have to prove it by getting your own knife wound? Not enough that I had one?" He grinned at her. She smiled back at him through her tears. Dylan grabbed his pack once more and turned before leaving the small cave. "Be careful, you two. I'll hurry back."

Felicia stood and hurried out after him. "Dylan?"

He turned to face her. Cupping her face in his hands, he gently kissed her. "You'll be all right. You and Natalie both have guns in your packs. Keep them handy. I'll be back shortly after daybreak. If something happens and I don't make it back, you pack up and head north. I'll find you. I love you, Felicia."

She nodded. "I'll be praying for you."

Dylan gave her a lop-sided smile. "It can't hurt. I'll be worrying about you, too." He kissed her again. "Try to get some sleep. Duke's a good watchdog. You'll be able to tell if something is wrong. Just watch his reaction." He looked back to see her still standing there as he mounted his horse and rode away.

"Come on," Natalie told her, putting her arms around her. "We'll pray together and then sleep. Dylan's right. Duke will wake us if he needs to."

"I'm not worried about us. I'm worried about Dylan. He's riding off alone with no one to help him if he needs it. I won't leave here until he gets back, Natalie. I won't."

Natalie pulled her gently into the cave. "He wouldn't leave without you either, honey."

Felicia was awakened by Duke's low growling as he lay next to her. She lay still, her ears straining to hear what it was that was bothering him. She put her hand underneath the blanket she had rolled up as a pillow until she closed her fingers around the handle of the pistol she had stored there. She wasn't leaving it unused in her pack any longer. Several seconds later, she bolted upright as a scream rent the morning air. By this time, Duke's growls had turned into a frantic barking. Now, Natalie and the children were also awake.

"I think it's a cougar," Mark said, his arms around his sister.

"A cougar!"

"Or a mountain lion. We used to hear them sometimes when we

went camping with our dad. He told us that the more people move up here and start living in and around the forest, the more we crowd the cougars. Black bears, too."

"Bears!" Felicia gasped. "We've already had enough of those. Hush, Duke!"

"We're all right. It won't come around the fire." Mark looked over to where the fire had burned down. "Someone needs to get more wood, though." He straightened his shoulders. "I'll go. With Dylan gone, I'm the man around here."

Natalie smiled. "I don't think so. I'll go. I'll take Duke with me, and my gun and a flashlight. I won't go far from this cave though, I can tell you that." She gathered up the things she needed and grabbed hold of the dog's collar. "You stay here and watch out for Felicia and your sister." Mark nodded reluctantly.

While Natalie searched for wood, Felicia and the children sat as far back in their shelter as they could. Felicia held each of the children's hands in hers and began to pray. "Father, we thank you for your mighty and awesome creation, but we're not used to being thrust into the middle of it. Protect us through the rest of this night and watch out for Natalie and Dylan. In Jesus's name, Amen." Within minutes Natalie had returned, her arms loaded with wood.

"Told you I wouldn't have to go far. I think that cougar has gone too. Didn't see or hear anything." She dropped the wood on the ground and slowly added it to the fire. "Duke stayed calm the whole time. I tried to find the driest wood I could, but it's damp out there and this might smoke a bit."

"Just wait then. The sun's coming up. We'll dry the wood out until we need it tonight." Felicia went to stand in the overhang, searching anxiously for a sign of Dylan. The day passed slowly. The women tried to keep the kids occupied with gathering wood and skipping stones in the nearby creek, but they were all aware of how the time crawled by while they waited anxiously for Dylan to return. The dog would periodically look down the path in the direction Dylan had taken and whine before someone would quiet him. By dusk, Dylan had still not returned and the women's faces were etched with worry.

"Well," Felicia said, getting up from where she had been sitting. "I guess I'll take the kids down to the creek and fill up the canteens. We've got time before it gets too dark." She smiled at the two children, trying to seem confident. "That way we'll be ready to leave when Dylan gets back."

"Great idea!" Natalie told them. "I'll practice my campfire cooking and fix something hot for our dinner."

Felicia held the children's hands as they walked down to the creek. It was the time of evening when the light was just starting to go gray. The trees overhead formed a dark canopy and she was glad each time they stepped into a clearing. She did her best to keep the children talking, but couldn't resist peering into the dark bushes on each side of the path. Every rustle, every twig that snapped, every sound set her teeth on edge and she felt herself ready to bolt at any moment.

Once they reached the creek, she left the children playing a game of tag while she bent down to fill the canteen. Small fish darted around the neck of container. Suddenly, Lisa began screaming. Felicia looked up quickly to see a large mountain lion watching her from the other side of the narrow creek. She rose slowly, leaving the canteen lying on the bank. Mark clamped a hand over his sister's mouth to quiet her screams. Felicia looked around for a weapon to use and grabbed a long stick about as thick as her wrist. When she began to slowly back up towards the children, the cat bounded across the creek. Lisa resumed her hysterical screaming.

"Shut up!" Mark ordered, grabbing her by the arm. He turned to run back towards camp and the cat pounced to cut them off.

Felicia ran up to them, putting herself between the children and the animal. "Get out of here!" she screamed, brandishing the stick. The cat roared and tried to run around her. In each direction that the children ran, the cat would run to intercept, as if it were trying to herd them away from Felicia. Lisa's hysterics were making it difficult for her older brother to keep a grip on her arm to lead her away. Felicia tried desperately to stay between them and the stalking animal. The cat screamed again and Lisa fell to the ground and covered her ears, her screams subsiding into sobs.

135

"Oh, God," Felicia prayed as the animal roared again. She stepped forward and jabbed at the mountain lion with the stick. The animal roared and swiped out, raking her hand with its claws. She screamed and dropped the stick. The pain was intense and she faltered before reaching down to grab the stick. Her hand was slippery with blood and she was having a difficult time holding on to it. The animal continued to roar and Lisa rocked on her knees, beginning to scream again. Mark tried desperately to quiet her and pull her back to her feet. The boy was struggling to hold back his own tears as he wrestled with his sister. Both of the children's eyes were wide with fright.

Felicia wrapped her bleeding hand into the flannel shirt she wore and continued to shout orders for the animal to go away. She kept trying all the things she had read about in books, about trying to appear too large to the animal to be considered prey. *Obviously this animal wasn't following the rules*, she thought to herself. The animal suddenly switched its attention from the children to her and sprang, knocking her to the ground. She began to scream and kick at the cat as it stood over her. She flailed her arms frantically, keeping it from being able to get a grip on her. When she fell, Duke burst from the trees, barking furiously. The dog taunted the cat, trying to distract it from Felicia. He managed to stay just out of reach of its claws.

Felicia got slowly to her feet, using her fallen stick to lean on. Her legs were shaking so hard she was afraid she would fall again. "Duke! Here!" The dog ignored her command and continued to focus its attention on the cat. The dog would rushed in close and bound away while the cat swiped and screamed in anger. Felicia held tight to her stick and motioned for the two children to get behind her. They slowly began to back up towards the path that led back to camp.

"Felicia!" Dylan ran down the path, rifle in his hand. He stopped just short of the fighting cat and dog and aiming the rifle in the air, pulled the trigger. Startled, the cat stopped. Dylan fired again and the animal bound back across the creek and disappeared. "Duke, stay!" Dylan ordered as the dog started to chase after the escaping animal.

Dylan ran over to where Felicia had collapsed to her knees. At that time, Natalie emerged from the woods and with a worried glance over to where Dylan had folded his arms around Felicia, she ran over to the two children. She put an arm around each of them and began heading them back to camp. Lisa continued to cry, glancing repeatedly over her shoulder at Felicia.

"Are you okay?" Dylan asked anxiously. "Are you hurt?" He began running his hands down her arms. He cursed to himself when he saw her hand, the blood beginning to seep through the shirt she had wound around it. Gently he took her hand in his and slowly unwound the shirt. Her hand had been scratched deeply, rather than punctured. Dylan took the shirt down to the creek and soaked it in the cool water. He flung the dropped canteens around his neck and went back to gently wipe the blood from Felicia's hand. "Can you make it back? We need to clean this and put a bandage around it." He searched her face for signs of shock and seeing her shiver, took off his own shirt and placed it around her shoulders. "Come on, honey." He helped her to her feet.

Natalie was waiting anxiously for them back at the camp where she had wrapped the children in blankets and handed them both a plate of beans. She saw her daughter's bleeding hand and put her own hand to her mouth in shock. "Oh, God, Dylan! She's hurt! Did it bite her? Where?"

"It's not bad. No bite, just some deep scratches," he reassured her. "She's frightened more than anything. Do you think you could get the fire going?"

"I can do it," Mark spoke up. Dylan smiled at him and nodded. Mark hurried to the backpacks for matches and within minutes had coaxed a fire into burning brightly.

Dylan sat Felicia carefully by the fire and told Natalie to get a blanket and the first aid kit. "I'm sorry I was gone so long," he told Felicia. "When I saw you standing there facing down that cougar…" his voice trailed off. "Well, I just about lost it. I couldn't stand it if anything happened to you. I'm sorry I wasn't here sooner."

"I'm fine. Just scared. I thought you weren't coming back, Dylan. When I saw you standing there, all the fears I've been feeling today just overwhelmed me."

Natalie handed Dylan the first aid kit. Dylan tried to apply the ointment as gently as he could, but still the pain caused Felicia to draw in her breath sharply. "I'm sorry," he apologized. "I'll be as quick as I can." He handed her some aspirin. "This is all we have for pain." She tried to smile back and looked over at the children.

"You two all right?" They nodded. "I didn't even think," she mumbled as Dylan drew her close to his chest. "All I could do was try to keep it away from Mark and Lisa. If you hadn't gotten there when you did... I could feel its breath on me, Dylan."

"As soon as I got back, I heard Lisa screaming and saw Duke tear off toward the creek. Natalie was starting to go after him. I told her to stay, which she didn't," he smiled over at her. "I grabbed the rifle and took off after the dog. The last thing I expected to see was you on the ground with a cougar standing over you."

"I didn't think mountain lions attacked people," Natalie said.

"They don't usually. Especially, adults. Maybe it was after the children. Could have smelled the dog, might have a den close by. Who knows?" He stood up. "I've brought the warm coats for everyone. I'll get them off the horse."

"Man, that was something!" Mark exclaimed, coming over to peer at Felicia's hand. "Like something out of a movie! Does it hurt much?"

She smiled up at him. "A little. You were really brave out there, Mark. I'm proud of the way you looked after your sister."

"I was scared," Lisa said, climbing into Felicia's lap. "I'm sorry I cried."

Felicia pulled her close with her uninjured hand. "That's okay. I was scared, too. I think I might have even cried." She looked around at Dylan who was still favoring his arm, then at the new bandage showing under Natalie's shirt, and laughed. "You two are the only unwounded ones here. The rest of us have been stabbed, cut and scratched. I'd say you two were the strongest ones in this group."

"What took you so long, Dylan?" Felicia asked, as the two of them loaded up the horses the next morning.

"I'm sorry, Felicia. I made it to that little country store and saw that it was all locked up. It was well into the day by then, so I got curious. I tried peering into the windows and couldn't see anything. When I went around to the back, the door was ajar and I went in." He tightened the cinch on the saddle savagely. "The old man and his wife were dead. Lying on the floor with their throats slit. Luther's people at least tracked us as far as that store. I covered up my tracks and went farther north until I found another store. I called in an anonymous tip to the police and bought what we needed." He grabbed her and pulled her roughly to him. "When I heard Lisa screaming and Duke barking, I thought for sure Luther had you. When I didn't run into you guys on my way back, I was certain. You were told to leave, you know?"

"I know."

"I saw Michael, Felicia."

"What?"

"He was watching me from the edge of the woods when I came out of the store. He was laughing. We stared at each other for a minute, waiting to see if the other one was going to make a move. When I started off in his direction, he ran."

"He's following us," she stated.

Dylan nodded. "I'd say that he thinks you're still his responsibility. He's determined to be the one to bring you in."

She shivered. "I'm glad you're here."

He smiled and kissed the top of her head. "Me too. Ready to go?"

It took the group well into the next day before they approached the home where Dylan's mother's friend lived. The small house was situated in a clearing surrounded by tall pines and thick underbrush. A barn sat a small distance from the house and one of the doors had come loose, causing it to sway in the slight breeze. Five cows grazed in the field beside the barn. The house had a neglected look about it as they sat there in the safety of the trees, waiting for Dylan to decide if it was all right to proceed. His gaze swept the yard. Weeds were sprouting up in the flowerbeds and the grass was knee high. He frowned and motioned for the others to remain silent. He slid down from his horse and pulled the rifle from its holster.

Dylan checked the barn first. The hay in the stalls was dirty, and rancid feed sat in the feeders. He wrinkled his nose and proceeded cautiously into the dim recesses of the barn. He jumped and swung the rifle around as an orange tabby cat hissed and jumped from the hayloft. Dylan's anxiety grew as he left the barn and walked around to the back of the house.

He tried the back door, only to find it locked. He peered into the window. The furniture inside lay covered with white sheets. He frowned. Why would she leave this time of the year and leave the house in such disarray? With the barrel of his gun, he broke out one of the smaller panes of glass in the back door and sliding his arm in, unlocked it. He held the rifle in front of him as he walked through the house, checking to see whether someone was hiding in one of the back rooms.

The house was straightened and clean except for the layer of dust covering the surfaces that weren't protected by sheets. He checked the pantry and was surprised to discover that it was well stocked. Dylan than checked the refrigerator and saw that it was empty. Mildred must have gone on an extended vacation. He opened the front door and motioned for the others to come in.

"There's no one here, but it's got two dry bedrooms and food in the pantry. The electricity is on, so there's hot water, but let's not use the lights." Dylan checked to make sure that the curtains were tightly closed. "I don't want to advertise our presence here. Mark, take the horses on out to the barn and I'll be there in a minute."

Luther could feel his peace slipping away. They had lost her! The witch who had his daughter was gone. No bleep showed on the computer screen before him. They couldn't have discovered the chip! None of Luther's followers knew they were bugged. It was impossible. He slammed the cover down on the laptop computer and began to pace the room.

He mentally noted where they had last been tracked to, and knew that his people were waiting in the area around the little store they had visited. If they returned, he'd have them. He had suffered frustration after frustration trying to get his daughter back. It was time for progress. He was getting impatient. Maybe it was time to appease the gods again. He pushed the button that opened the curtains on the room of young girls. Yes…. That one would do nicely. Innocent and pure. Luther called in the man standing outside his door and ordered that everyone gather that evening for the ceremony and for them to have the young girl prepared. Luther smiled. A sacrifice such as she should turn favor once again in his direction.

He left his room and strolled leisurely around the grounds of his commune. The forest around the island had been allowed to grow thick so as to shelter them from prying eyes. From the far shore, or from a boat, the island looked overgrown and deserted. They felt they were safe from the outside world. Luther was content to allow the few outside people who did know about them, such as city officials, believe they were a harmless religious commune, living off the land and their own survival skills. The lease for the land was listed under a false identity. He felt he had covered his tracks well.

He walked among his people as if he were invisible. No one dared to acknowledge his presence, unless he acknowledged them first. He was truly the master here. Even the children were learning to cast down their eyes when he strolled by. Yes, with his daughter's fate complete, he would know power beyond his wildest imagination. He smiled to himself then felt a moment's remorse that the mother of his daughter could not rule by his side and shook his head. There was no room in his life for weakness. She would have to die for betraying him.

As night began to fall, Luther made his way back to his room to prepare for the ceremony ahead. All his adult followers were required to attend. It was mandatory and failure to do so was punished severely.

After donning his hooded robe, Luther left his room and was pleased to see his people walking towards the door that led to the underground ceremonial. His sharp eye told him that all were accounted for. His commune housed fifty adults and slightly fewer children, not counting the abductees. He let a rare smile flit across his face. Yes, his reward in eternity would be great indeed.

Chapter 17

It wasn't until the morning of the third day that the little group's rest was disturbed. They had helped themselves to the food in the pantry, venturing outside only to care for the horses. They kept the shades drawn tight and did as Dylan had suggested by keeping to candlelight. When Dylan rose that morning, he was pleased to be feeling a lot less pain when he flexed his arm. He peered carefully through the curtains and was surprised to see that it had snowed during the night and the snow was still falling lightly. Good, they would stay until the snow stopped. He sniffed and smelled the pleasing aroma of coffee and bacon.

"Good morning. See the snow?" he asked, walking into the kitchen.

"It's beautiful." Felicia stood by the stove. "We found bacon in a freezer behind the pantry and Natalie took the off chance that maybe your friend kept a couple of chickens. She did. There's a little chicken coop not far from the barn. She found it when she went out to feed the horses this morning."

"Sounds great. It'll be a welcome change, that's for sure. Kids up?"

"They're getting up and Natalie is in the shower. I'll have all this done up in a minute." Dylan sat back in one of the kitchen chairs and watched her work. He noticed that the bandage on her hand was gone. Good. They were all healing. Felicia had pulled her hair back from her face with a piece of ribbon and had donned a heavy sweater and a pair of overalls. He hadn't thought she had overalls with her. Looking down he noticed that she had rolled them up to just below her knees. *Must be a pair of Mildred's,* he thought. *They're too short for her. She sure does look good in them,* he noted to himself.

"What?"

"Huh?" Dylan glanced back up, trying unsuccessfully to hide his smile.

"What's so funny?"

"Nothing."

"Something is. Do I look funny? I just wanted to be comfortable today and I found these in the closet. They're warm."

"You look beautiful."

Felicia smiled shyly and turned back to the stove as Natalie followed the children into the kitchen.

"Mmmm. Smells great!" Mark announced, plopping himself in a chair.

"Perfect timing. Breakfast is served." Felicia dished out the eggs and bacon and tossed a couple of slices to Duke. When they were finished, Felicia sent the two children to wash the dishes and then refilled the adults' coffee.

"Well," Dylan said after taking a sip. "It looks like we can leave here tomorrow, if the snow lets up. My arm is doing fine. Felicia's hand is apparently better. What about you, Natalie?"

Before she could answer, Dylan realized that Duke was standing at attention looking towards the front room. Dylan told him to be quiet before the dog had a chance to bark. "Get Mark and Lisa," he whispered to Felicia. "Natalie, get your gun and we'll all meet back in here. Hopefully, it's just a neighbor checking on the cows." The women nodded and within minutes they were all gathered silently in the kitchen.

Dylan held set his rifle against the wall and with his revolver in his hand, walked cautiously into the front room where he could get a good view of the front yard. His fears were confirmed. Two men stood quietly conversing near the front porch. Both were dressed in snow-white snowsuits with their faces hidden beneath ski masks. Both men carried nine-millimeter handguns. These weren't helpful neighbors. Keeping low, Dylan made his way back to the kitchen.

"There are two men outside. They're searching. I don't think they know for certain that we're here but it won't take them long to figure it out. I want Mark and Lisa to hide in the pantry. Felicia, take my pistol and get down on the floor in the front room. Natalie, you go with her. Neither one of you shoot until you hear from me. You'll be able to distinguish my rifle over their automatics."

"Automatics?" Felicia asked in horror.

Dylan nodded. "It's going to take all three of us to bring these guys down. I'm sending the dog after the kids. Mark, you keep him quiet and Lisa, no crying whatsoever. It's important that we all remain very, very quiet. okay?" The children nodded and scooted themselves backwards to the pantry. "You two position yourselves by these two windows. Don't shoot unless you have a clear shot and stay down as much as possible. Do your best not to let *anyone* in this house. If I'm able to come back in, I'll announce myself. Otherwise shoot anyone who comes through that door. I'm going to try and sneak around and get behind them." Natalie nodded and checked the ammunition in her gun. She pulled her bag from underneath the coffee table where she had stashed it and grabbed another box of ammo and she tossed one to Felicia.

"Sweetheart? You okay? I know this is going to be hard for you. Just remember what I taught you." Dylan searched Felicia's face.

She nodded and set her mouth into a firm line. "I'm tired of running, Dylan. I'm ready." He gave her a quick kiss and disappeared quietly out the back door. The two women quietly said a quick prayer together and took their positions beneath the window. Natalie jumped up quickly and disappeared into the kitchen, returning with an ice pick in her hand. She smiled at Felicia and mouthed, "Just in case". Felicia stared at her for a second before turning her attention back to the window. They both jumped in alarm as the front door handle wiggled. They backed up against the far wall, holding their weapons out in front of them, and waited for Dylan's signal.

The snow was falling harder when Dylan made his way outside. The flakes were full and fat enough to make visibility hard. It was still early enough in the morning that the light had a grayish tinge to it. *Good,* he thought. At least the light won't bounce off the snow and blind me. I'm sure not dressed for this. He looked down at the jeans he wore and his sweater. He hadn't thought to grab his parka. He made his way hurriedly into the woods bordering the property, being careful to not step on any frozen twigs and give himself away. He walked around to where he could see the front porch. The two men were trying to get into the house. Dylan swirled around as he heard a vehicle driving up the lane. He was shocked to see Michael emerge from behind the wheel.

"Felicia! It's me, Michael!" He approached the two men on the front porch. "Have you confirmed that they are in there?" Michael strode right up to the front door and tried the handle. "We don't want to waste our time if they're not here."

Felicia choked off a scream as one of the men shoved his elbow through the glass pane of the window in front her.

"Confirmation enough?" the man asked.

"Felicia! Don't make us do this the hard way! Come on out!" Michael paced the porch, trying to peer in through the closed curtains. He cursed when she didn't answer and jumped down from the porch.

Within seconds, one of the other men had thrust his hand inside and was reaching for the doorknob. Immediately, Natalie snatched up the ice pick and buried it in his hand. The man howled and drew back. The other man rushed forward to try and kick the door down just as Dylan's first shot rang out. His bullet took the man in the leg, dropping him, but not stopping him. The two women quickly moved back to the windows and began to shoot. The two men dove for cover off the porch. Michael sprinted back to his truck yelling over his shoulder as he ran, "No accidents, boys! She had better come out of this alive or it's your hides Luther will be after!" He backed down the drive, spraying gravel as Dylan's shots came close to his tires.

The other men were undecided on whether they should open fire on the woods behind them, or on the house. Dylan and the two women held their fire. The men had a good cover behind the bushes that ran the length of the porch.

Dylan remained crouched and shivering under the dripping trees, waiting for the men to make another move. He lay his gun down momentarily and blew on his hands, trying to warm them. He needed the flexibility in order to aim and fire efficiently.

One of them raised his head to peer around and Natalie squeezed off a shot, causing him to duck back down with a shriek. The two men opened fire on the house. Natalie and Felicia threw themselves down on their bellies and crawled back towards the kitchen. Dylan stood and squeezed off two shots in succession, trying to draw the men's fire to him. One man turned his gun in the direction of the woods and Dylan dove for cover, deciding to wait until the other man made a mistake and gave him an open target. His patience wore off and Dylan's next shot took the man in the chest as his comrade crashed through the bullet-riddled door.

Natalie shoved Felicia into the kitchen as the man came through the front door, causing the younger women to fall and slide across the floor. Natalie held her gun at the ready and went forward to meet their attacker.

"Natalie, no!" Felicia grabbed the gun she had dropped and rushed back into the living room. Natalie was too close to the man for him to draw up his weapon and shoot her, so instead he was trying to push her back and club her with it. She scrambled around him and climbed up his back, hanging on with her arms tightly around his neck. He tried reaching up behind him and bashing her with his gun, to no avail. Suddenly, he ducked and Natalie found herself on her back on the floor. As he leveled the gun at Natalie's head, Felicia took aim and pulled the trigger. The man looked over at her in surprise before looking down at the quickly spreading red stain across his chest. Natalie kicked the gun out of his hand and shoved him to the floor as Dylan burst through the front door.

He glanced quickly around the room, his eyes searching for Felicia. He saw her standing in the door leading to the kitchen, her face frozen in shock. The gun slid from her fingers and hit the floor. The sound seemed abnormally loud as the weapon bounced on the wooden floor. Seeing that Natalie was all right, Dylan stepped over the dead man and made his way to Felicia. He pulled her tenderly into his arms and laid her head against his chest. They stood there silently as

Natalie walked around them to let the children out of their hiding place.

"Is he dead?" Felicia raised her stricken face. "He was going to kill Natalie."

"Shhh. Everything is fine. We're safe for now." He smoothed the hair that had fallen from its ribbon, back from her face. "Are you hurt?"

She shook her head. "Dylan, Michael was out there. He was one of those men."

"He got away. Once the shooting started, he ran. Probably to get more help."

They both turned to see Natalie and the children watching them. Mark's eyes were wide as he took in the dead man lying in the living room and the legs of the man lying across the threshold. Lisa was silently crying, the tears coursing down her cheeks. Felicia made a valiant effort to pull herself together and went to kneel before them. "It's all right now. You two were great at hiding. Not a sound."

"We were scared when the shooting started," Mark told her. "But Lisa promised not to make any noise. She didn't, either!"

"Good job. Both of you." Dylan looked again at the two dead men. "Let's get rid of these two. Natalie, once again I'm asking for some of your cash. I'll leave a note for Mildred. We've got a lot of riding ahead of us. Do you all think you can do it now, or would you rather wait until morning?"

"I don't want to sleep another night here," Felicia said, looking at the two men.

"I agree," Natalie added. "We stopped too close to where we got rid of the chip. It was too easy for them to find us. I don't know how many more of them could be out there waiting for these two to return and we can be pretty certain that Michael will return with more, and soon. I'll help you move these two guys and Felicia and the children can pack things up."

Dylan heaved up one of the men and slung him across his shoulders. His legs buckled momentarily under the weight, then he steadied himself. Natalie grabbed the legs of the man already outside and together they managed to drag them to the back of the barn. Dylan rolled the bodies into a dry well that he had discovered the day before.

"Should we let Mildred know that there are two bodies in her old well?"

Dylan shrugged. "What do we tell her? Hey, by the way we killed a couple of guys and tossed them in your well? The well is dry now. Just put the cover back on and nail it down."

"Good point. I'll go start getting rid of any evidence they might have left behind. Their weapons might be useful."

"There are a couple of backpacks stashed by the porch. Go through those while I saddle the horses."

Natalie dragged the two packs into the kitchen and tossed them onto the table. She found a small variety of dry foods, some ammunition and one of the guys had a hunting knife. She repacked all they could use into one of the bags and threw out the other. Felicia and the children had piled the rest of their belongings on the porch outside and Felicia had changed back into her own clothes. She glanced over at the small pile of money that Natalie had left on the table.

"At this rate, we're going to run out of money. We're always having to pay for damages."

"Thank you."

"For what?"

"For saving me. I know how hard that must have been for you to pull that trigger."

"I didn't even think. I saw that he was going to kill you and I reacted. But... you're welcome." The two women smiled at each other and carried out the last of their things. Dylan had just brought the horses around and the children were handing him things while he tied them onto the extra horse.

"Well... on the road again," Mark said seriously.

The rest of them laughed as they mounted the horses and Dylan led them back into the forest.

Chapter 18

Several days of slow travel, because of children and snow, finally brought the group to within a half-mile of Bloody Island. Dylan warned everyone to remember to be alert at all times and as quiet as possible. Felicia groaned silently as she finally slid from her horse in front of an abandoned shed that Dylan had discovered. She ached in every part of her body. She untied the pack from her horse and grunting, hoisted it up and carried it inside.

The shed had been kept unlocked and a thick film of dust covered every available surface. It was hard to tell what had once been stored here but they could see that it had been home to a number of small animals. Natalie and the children were already trying to sweep some of the dust out with branches and were sneezing in the process. The few windows the shed had were long since broken and Dylan set to work finding something to cover them with. Felicia dropped her pack and sat on it, putting her chin in her hands.

"I ache all over. What I wouldn't give for a nice hot bath."

"Doesn't look like we'll be getting anything hot for a while yet," Natalie told her. "We're too close to Luther to risk a fire."

"I'll go out in the morning and scout around," Dylan told them. "Once I've located him exactly, I'll call in to my old precinct and get some help. If they won't help, I've got some people who owe me a favor. I'll get someone out here to watch Mark and Lisa and we'll hunt for Luther." He motioned for Felicia to get up and then picked up her pack. "Stop swishing the dust around, kids. We'll just have to lay our packs on the ground. We can gather up evergreen branches to put between us and the dirt if you want, but that sweeping is making it difficult to breathe." Dylan tossed the packs into the corner. "Natalie, take those two outside to hunt up our makeshift beds and Felicia and I will try and organize in here. Take your gun." She nodded and ushered the children outside.

"You, okay?"

Felicia looked over. "Sure. Why wouldn't I be?"

"We're close to the end now. The proverbial pooh is going to be hitting the fan soon, as they say."

She smiled. "Really. I'm as surprised as you are, but I feel perfectly fine. Maybe I'm just too tired to be worried right now. We've had a peaceful few days. It's a little harder for them to track us without my mother's little device."

"Your mother?" Dylan sounded surprised.

"Yeah," she answered sheepishly. "With all we've been through I think it's time to acknowledge the fact that she *is* my mother. I've actually come to care for her a great deal. I'm looking forward to having a relationship with her when this is all over."

"That sounds great! I know of another relationship I'd like to pursue."

Felicia blushed and bowed her head. "Dylan."

Natalie, Mark, and Lisa reentered the shed with their arms loaded down with evergreen branches. The kids were smiling and whispering as they proceeded to make up five piles of the branches. "I think it did them good to walk around a bit," Natalie said smiling. She tossed her head to the side for Dylan and Felicia to join her outside. They looked at each other and followed her out.

"What?"

"This is a pretty populated place, Dylan. While the kids and I were out, I spotted several different sets of footprints."

"Tourists?"

"I don't think so. The footprints stayed mainly to a path, but several branched out into the bushes. They didn't all look like hiking boot tracks to me."

"Tourists using the restroom."

"No. It's a feeling I have. I know we're close to Luther's place, but I think this shed may have been used by him at one time or another. The prints weren't fresh," she said, anticipating Dylan's next question.

"I'll hike as far as the lake tomorrow. See if I can't find out for sure if Bloody Island is his home. For now, we'll eat more cold food and try to get a good night's sleep. Okay?"

The two women nodded and followed him back into the shed. By this time their sleeping bags had been laid across the piles of branches.

"Why, it looks just like home," Felicia told the beaming children. "I can't wait to lie down on them."

"I can't wait to sleep in a real bed again," Mark told her.

"Me either," Lisa added. "I'm tired of the ground."

"Come on, you two. Here's some granola bars and juice. We're eating at the Ritz tonight. Let's pretend, shall we, that we're at a fancy hotel and restaurant." Felicia handed out their dinner. Mark and Lisa took the food from her with frowns.

"Again?" they whined in unison.

"Again," Natalie told them. "Go sit on your beds to eat. And then it's straight to sleep. We can't light a fire so we need to sleep when the sun goes down." The three adults sat in the dark for several more hours as they planned the next day. Dylan tried to lay out his plans the best he could without drawing things in the dirt, hoping they knew what to do if he should not make it back tomorrow.

Dylan left the next morning on foot, leaving before the others were awake. He was uncomfortable leaving them alone again but he knew he could travel much faster and quieter alone. He stayed off the beaten paths as much as possible, keeping low in the thick undergrowth.

By noon he had reached the bank of the lake and lay belly flat on the ground under the thickest bushes he could find. He noticed only one dilapidated building and it was hidden fairly well by overgrown bushes. The island looked abandoned to anyone viewing it. He waited for someone, or something, to move on the island.

After about an hour his patience was rewarded. Two men came out of a door in the ground and walked about fifty feet before seeming to disappear underground again. Well, an apparently deserted island with underground buildings that no one knows about. Seems like someone is hiding something, he told himself. He scooted backwards until he was out from under the bush and dusted himself off before heading back to the shed where he had left the others.

The shed was empty. The horses were still tied in the trees out of sight of the shed and the backpacks were still inside where they had left them but Natalie, Felicia and the children were gone. Feeling a sense of panic, Dylan gripped his rifle tighter and began studying the ground. He found their footprints easily and saw others mixed in. The footprints were all messed and unclear. As if there had been some struggling. He felt the icy grip of fear take hold of him. He checked to be sure he still had his knife, grabbed the backpack he always carried, and took off back towards the lake at a run.

It was early evening before Dylan smelled the smoke of a campfire. He slowed down his pace and approached cautiously in the direction he thought the smoke was coming. Again, he resorted to belly crawling. As he parted the bushes in front of him he had to hold himself back as he saw Natalie struggling in the grips of two men. Several men stood around them and others were piling wood to make a larger fire. Standing a few feet past Natalie was a tall, bald man dressed all in black. Luther! And next to him, a satisfied smirk on his face as he watched Natalie struggle, was Michael. Felicia and the children were sitting on the ground behind Luther, gagged, with their hands and feet tied. Dylan saw Luther say something to the two men who held Natalie and she yelled back at him, but Dylan couldn't make out what was being said. Michael walked forward and slapped Natalie hard enough to throw her head back and cause her mouth to bleed.

While Dylan watched in horror, he saw the men drag the struggling woman over to where a large mound of wood was piled and then tie her to a stake raised in the middle of it. She looked over at Felicia and yelled something again. Dylan could see Felicia struggling against her ties and the two children were crying. As if she knew that he was there, Natalie looked to where Dylan was hidden and nodded solemnly. She raised her eyes to heaven as he watched a man take a burning log from the smaller fire and light the kindling around her feet.

Dylan released the safety on his gun and peered down the barrel to begin picking off Luther's men. His first shot took out one of the men who had tied the rope around Natalie's hands. "Dylan!" Natalie screamed. "You can't get them all! You know what you have to do! Just make it quick... please!" Without thinking, and with tears streaming down his face, Dylan swung the barrel around and squeezed the trigger. Felicia began screaming through her gag and struggling to rise. One of the men standing near her knocked her back to the ground.

As Natalie's head fell forward in death, Dylan turned and ran, dodging bullets. He realized that he was outnumbered and knew he was going to have to turn back and follow them, trying to remain undetected. Tree branches blocked his path and he switched directions once again. He realized he wasn't being followed and fell to his knees, allowing the sobs to wrack his body.

He raised his head and howled, "Why? She loved you... She believed in you!" He let himself fall farther until he lay prostrate on the damp ground. As he lay prone amongst the decaying leaves and moist soil, he felt the savage sobs begin to lessen and he felt himself begin to experience the peace that Natalie had demonstrated in her life... and in her death.

For the first time in many years, Dylan realized he wasn't alone in his quest. That someone had been walking by his side the entire time. Although his sorrow over Natalie's death was still raw, he began to believe that she was now safely home in the arms of the Father she loved. He sniffed and wiped the tears from his eyes.

There among the wildness of the forest, still able to smell the smoke from the fire drifting on the breeze, Dylan bent his head and met his Savior.

Chapter 19

A group of men, including Michael, stormed the small shed early that morning as the women and children were having their scanty breakfast. Felicia looked up to see a tall, thin man watching them from the doorway.

"Luther," Natalie whispered, as she bolted for her gun.

"I wouldn't," Luther said calmly. "We don't want to engage in gun fire here. Our daughter, or one of these lovely children, could be harmed."

Natalie stood and faced him. "So... you found us."

Luther clasped his hands behind his back. "Wasn't too difficult, my dear. Although getting rid of the chip *was* a smart move on your part. I haven't given you enough credit, but by that time we had you under pretty constant surveillance." He walked over to the two children and caressed their faces. "So young and innocent." He turned to stand before Felicia. "My daughter. We finally meet. You are as beautiful as I always knew you would be." He reached out to touch her and she pulled back, disgust marring her features. Luther frowned, his eyes growing cold. He motioned for the other men to come in. "Tie them up. We've got to get out of here before our *hero* returns. If he comes back early, kill him." With those words, Luther spun on his heels and left the building.

Felicia looked up at Michael standing in the doorway. "How could you do this to us? We grew up together."

"We had some fun together, Felicia. That was all. You looked good hanging on my arm, but this," he waved his arm towards Luther. "This is your destiny. I was just helping you to it." He nodded for the men to continue rounding them up.

The women and children struggled in vain. They knew they were no match for these men. Lisa cried silently as Mark was separated from her. The walk to the bonfire didn't take long. They were dragged roughly through the forest, branches grabbing at their hair and clothing. Once they reached the clearing, Natalie was taken from them and they were shoved roughly to the ground.

"Watch, my dear," Luther told Felicia. "See what happens to those who leave my flock and betray me. I let your mother into my very being, and this is how she repaid me."

Felicia watched in horror as the men pushed Natalie around. Her mother's eyes filled with pain and anger when Michael slapped her. She knew that she and the children were safe for now, and inside her heart she knew Natalie's moments on this earth were running out. Luther had no need for her to live. Felicia tried bargaining with him but he ignored her as if she hadn't spoken.

When Natalie shouted into the woods across from them and Felicia saw the first man fall under Dylan's bullet, her fear for Dylan threatened to overwhelm her. She didn't expect the shot to ring forth, killing Natalie, and she screamed against the gag in her mouth. Tears spilled forth and ran down Felicia's cheeks as Natalie slumped forward against the ropes that bound her to the stake. Felicia raised her eyes to Luther, hate and tears blinding her. She struggled against her own bonds, wanting to kill this man. Luther saw the hate on her face.

"Patience, my child. I have greater things in store for you." He turned to where the fire was growing stronger. "Let the witch burn." He looked in the direction that Dylan's shots had come from. "Let's get these others back to our camp before their friend gets any more foolish ideas." He turned away and a handful of his followers escorted Felicia and the children away, while the others remained behind, shooting into the forest.

Luther had small motorboats waiting at the lake's shore and hurried everyone in them. Felicia scanned the bank behind them as the small boats roared across the lake. She kept hoping for a glimpse of Dylan to let her know he was safe.

Within minutes they were landing on the shore of the island. Mark put up a valiant fight as he was lifted from the boat and slumped unconscious as one of the men knocked him alongside his head. Lisa screamed against her gag and sagged against Felicia. She didn't struggle when one of the men lifted her out of the boat. Felicia stared coldly at the man who grabbed her arm, and jerked away. She stood proudly and exited on her own accord. She was handed over to a small group of women and led away into one of the underground buildings. She glanced over her shoulder and watched silently as the children were carried into another building.

One of the women withdrew a large copper key from her pocket and opened a steel door in front of them. Another women removed Felicia's gag and the ropes that were still binding her wrists. Gently, they pushed her into the room and locked the door after her.

"Wait!" Felicia called after them. "Help me! Please!" Receiving no answer, she looked around her. The small cell, in which she was being held had no furniture except a small cot. A thin blanket lay folded across one end. There was no window and the only view out of the cell was a small barred area cut into the locked door. She turned back to it. "Help! Someone! Anyone!" She slumped against the door and felt the tears begin to flow again. "I've got to stop this," she said to herself. "I've got to concentrate on getting myself out of here."

Felicia lay on the cot for what felt like several hours before she heard a key turning in the door. She sat up, her back against the wall. Three women entered, all wearing white robes, no expression on their faces. Two of them grabbed her arms and held her tightly while the third withdrew a hypodermic needle from a hidden pocket in her robes and plunged it into Felicia's arm. She fell back on the cot, her limbs growing heavy. She watched the three women as they seemed to move in slow motion. They began undressing her and she opened her mouth to protest but no words came. She had lost her ability to move or speak. A solitary tear ran down her check and onto the cot beneath her. She closed her eyes and turned her head, while the women finished their preparations.

Dylan reached the bank of Clear Lake as Felicia and the others were being unloaded on the other side. He had outrun the men left behind to search for him and he backtracked and waited until he saw them rejoin Luther on the other side of the lake. He quickly scanned the surrounding area for a boat and finding one, his first reaction was to jump aboard it and rush to the other side. As he thought about it, he decided to hide until dark and row himself across. The boat was a small, two-man rowboat and he realized that rowing would be quieter than an engine. Surprise was his greatest weapon. Mentally, he ran down the list of supplies he had in his backpack. A tear gas grenade, knife, 357 Magnum, the rifle he held in his hand and spare ammunition.

He stepped back into the cover of the trees. If he was going to save Felicia and the children he had to come up with a plan. He would call in some of his old buddies from the force. It would take them a few hours to get there but he knew they would be willing to help him out once he explained the situation. Dylan hoisted his pack back onto his shoulder, hid the rifle in a fallen log and set off at a quick pace for town. He needed to make a phone call.

He was frantic by the time he returned to the lake. It had taken him longer to take care of things in town and it was now several hours into the night. He had managed to get a hold of one of his friends who promised to contact as many of the others as he could. They wouldn't be able to contact him as to when they would be there. Dylan just prayed it would be in time. Since Dylan was acting outside of the police force, he could only rely on friends who also were no longer active police officers. He would worry about the red tape once Felicia was safe and then the authorities could have Luther.

He quickly set his gear in the small boat and pushed off from the bank. His plan was to try and rescue Felicia and the children with as little death as possible. His newly found faith made the idea of killing someone much less desirable than it once had been. His mind ran over his plan several times before he reached the other side. His plan was hastily made and full of holes. Dylan knelt in the boat before getting out and prayed for God's help. "Help me, Lord. This woman is precious to me and her life is at stake. Help me, please. Guide my hand and give me wisdom. Amen."

He sat still for a moment until he felt peace, then he pushed the boat up onto the shore. He saw only a couple of people wandering the grounds. One of them was a woman. Dressed in the dark clothes he had purchased while in town, Dylan blended into the shadow. He once again hoisted up his pack and rifle and set off quietly for one of the doors he could spot in the ground not far from him. He tried staying as close to the tree line as possible, not wanting to attract attention. He was the only person out there who wasn't wearing a robe and was carrying a gun and backpack. Several times he found himself stepping farther into the trees as someone approached closer than he was comfortable with. All those heading towards the underground building kept their faces pointed straight ahead, not looking to the left or the right. Dylan breathed a sigh of relief as the last person disappeared underground, pulling the door shut behind them.

The door groaned slightly as he lifted it and he stopped, listening. Not hearing anyone sounding an alarm or heading in his direction, he entered the dim stairwell leading down. About thirty feet in front of him, the hall split into a T-junction. Dylan looked in both directions. The way to the right was a long hall that led to a single room.

Dylan peered down the dark hall then decided to turn left. Several doors lead off this hallway in both directions. He quickly began peering into the small barred windows and was dismayed to see many children locked in each room. Some of the rooms held only young women. Beginning to be alarmed that he wouldn't find any of the three he was looking for, he started to turn around and head down the hall in the other direction.

"Dylan. Over here," Mark whispered from the last room on Dylan's right. Dylan hurried over to the door.

"Is Felicia in there with you?"

"No. It's just me and Lisa. They never brought Felicia down here."

Dylan glanced down and saw that the door only opened from his side. Quickly, he pushed the door open and gathered Mark and Lisa in his arms. He held up a finger to silence the little girl when she started to speak. "I'm taking you to the small boat I have hidden. Can you row, Mark?" The boy nodded. "Quietly, follow me." He scooped Lisa up and hurried back the way he had come.

"What about all the others?" Mark whispered. "We have to help them, too."

"I've got help coming. When they get here, we'll help everyone. I promise. Right now I'm taking care of you." He rushed them to the boat and helped them in. "Row quickly to the other side. Felicia and I will find a way to join you later. Don't stop for anyone and hide, Mark. I mean it. Really, really hide. Can you do that?"

The boy nodded and Dylan gave them a shove off the bank. He watched them for only a minute before turning and heading off in the direction that Mark had said Felicia was taken. He prayed again that he wasn't too late.

Chapter 20

In readiness for the ceremony, scheduled to take place shortly after midnight, Luther began the ritual of consecrating himself. He had fasted and prayed for days in anticipation of his daughter's return and needed only the few hours left to finalize his dedication. He stripped off all his clothing and began to methodically cleanse every inch of his body with the purifying solution he had prepared earlier that day. This, he had kept locked in a cabinet which only he had the key to. In doing this, he was guaranteed that the cleansing solution would remain pure.

With the cleansing process completed, Luther laid out on his bed the black and red robes he would wear. On top of these, he laid a black, jewel-handled knife. He had saved it especially for tonight. With his preparations done, he sat, still naked, upon the only chair in his room and immersed himself in prayer.

Dylan was half way across the main grounds of the commune when he heard movement ahead of him. He threw himself to the ground and peered through the dark ahead of him. Maybe thirty people were walking across the grounds, dressed in flowing black robes. Four of them carried a stretcher between them. Dressed in a startling white robe, her dark hair flowing down and over the sides of the stretcher, lay Felicia. She appeared to be unconscious, yet her eyes were open.

Dylan held his breath as the group passed to just a few feet of where he lay hidden. His first reaction was to stand up and start firing away with his guns, like a hero of the old westerns he was fond of, but common sense had him stay quietly where he was and wait for a better opportunity. His eyes narrowed when one of the robed figures turn right and he made out Michael's profile.

He watched as they entered the same underground tunnels he had just rescued Mark and Lisa from. He crept quietly around to the back of the mound and watched as the group disappeared underground. Startled, Dylan whipped around as another black-robed figure walked close to where he was. He stepped back into the bushes and stepped on a dry twig. Dylan froze until the man started to turn towards the sound. Within seconds, Dylan had pounced on the robed man, knocked him unconscious and transferred the robe the man wore to his own body. He hid the guns and grenade in the pockets under the robe and hurried down into the dark tunnels.

He could see that the group ahead of him turned right at the T-junction ahead and he hurried to catch up with them. He stayed just a few steps behind them and kept his head down. He prayed that God would help him remain undetected as the crowd entered a large room.

Dylan raised only his eyes and peered around. The only light in the large room were from candles that were lined up around the walls. One large candelabrum stood in the center of the room next to a large marble table. The four people carrying the stretcher that contained Felicia approached the table, and helped her stand. Still without speaking, they lifted her and lay her upon the top of the table and carefully arranged her robes and hair around her. Dylan could tell that Felicia had been drugged. Her neck was wobbly and she had trouble standing under her own power.

Another of the robed figures walked the circumference of the room lighting additional candles, and then he approached a small brazier next to the table where Felicia lay. The brazier began to give off a strong scent that quickly became overpowering in the closed room. Dylan tried breathing as shallow as possible.

Michael stood at the head of the marble table, supervising the preparations. He stood silently with his hands crossed and hidden in the sleeves of his robe. Another person carried up a small table on which lay a wooden box. This person opened the box and removed a single black-handled dagger. Dylan chanced raising his head higher and looked around for Luther. He had still not chosen to make his appearance. He began to fear that his help would be late and he would have to attempt Felicia's rescue on his own.

Dylan began to notice that people on either side of him were beginning to sway and he was alarmed to find himself growing dizzy. He turned his head to try breathing through the hood of his robe but found he wasn't able to see what was taking place in the room with his head turned. He took a deep breath from inside the protection of his hood and turned his head slightly so he could see. If he could keep a clear mind, the fact that the others were succumbing to the fumes of the incense would work to his advantage.

As if knowing exactly when the preparations were complete, Luther entered the room from a door at the far end. He wore a black silk robe trimmed in red with no hood. Looking only in front of him, he slowly approached the altar where Felicia lay. He began to speak in a language that Dylan did not understand. As time went on, Dylan could see that Luther was working himself into frenzy, and the swaying of the others in the room also grew in intensity. Dylan began to pray. As the others chanted under their breaths around him, Dylan prayed quietly to the only God that would be able to save him and give him the strength to save Felicia.

He was surprised by a robed Michael standing before him, patiently holding out a goblet in the shape of a human skull. Inside the goblet was a drink that looked like blood. Dylan had been praying with his eyes closed and was taken aback to see that a young girl had been tied to a post in the center of the room and the goblet appeared to contain the blood from a wound in her side. He realized that he was expected to drink from this. Repulsed, he took the goblet and raised it to his lips, pretending to drink.

Apparently Michael was satisfied with this, and not recognizing Dylan in the gloom of the room, took the goblet back, and proceeded around the circle. With this accomplished, Luther picked up the dagger on the table beside him and approached Felicia. With his voice rising in volume and intensity he raised it above his head.

Dylan slipped his hand beneath his robes and fumbled for a smoke grenade. Holding his breath, he pulled the ring and tossed the grenade to the center of the room. As the smoke quickly filled the room and shocks of alarm rang, Dylan rushed to where Felicia lay.

"Stop! You don't know what you're doing!" Luther stood there, seeming to be unaffected by the smoke and fumes. He still had the dagger raised, only this time he was aiming it in Dylan's direction. Dylan's lungs began to burn from holding his breath and he withdrew his revolver.

"I'm taking her out of here."

"You have defiled this place, young man. The penalty for that is death."

Michael whipped a small pistol from inside his robe and aimed it at Dylan. "I'll kill you before you reach the door."

"You cannot fire that gun in here!" Luther was dismayed to see all his preparations falling around him. "You might hit her. She can only die by my hand."

Dylan grabbed Felicia around the waist and dragged her off the table. He began to cough from the fumes. Without lowering his gun, he hoisted her over his shoulder and backed away from Luther. He could see others beginning to become aware of him and tried to hurry. Hands reached out to try and grab Felicia from him and he struck out with the gun and his feet. Sometimes, he connected with someone through the smoke and felt the satisfaction of them pulling back. His eyes began to burn and he kept blinking to try and rid them of the tears that were threatening to blind him. He continued to struggle through the room and could hear Luther ordering his people to stop them. Michael was making his way around the perimeter of the room, trying to get there in time to cut them off. Dylan fired into the air and the others pulled back.

Upon reaching the door he flung it open and propped Felicia against the wall. He looked around for something with which to barricade the door. Seeing one of the empty cells, hurried inside. He quickly dragged the cot over to the door and stuck it under the door handle. Looking up, he saw Michael glaring at him through the smoky window.

He couldn't make out what he was saying, but he knew that Michael was angry.

The physical exertion set him to coughing again and he bent under the onslaught of it. Felicia moaned and began to flutter her eyes. "Felicia," he whispered between coughs. "Can you hear me? Can you get up?" The pounding grew louder on the other side of the door.

She moaned again and slumped over. Dylan wiped his streaming eyes on his sleeve and crawled to her side. The pounding continued to increase and he saw that the door wasn't going to hold much longer. Michael was now shooting his gun at the door handle. Grunting with the effort, he slung the unconscious girl over his shoulder once more and struggled to run under her weight. They reached the top of the stairs when he heard the door fall. The robed figures were no longer silent and he could hear their angry shouts chasing after them. He burst through the door into the fresh air and stopped momentarily to draw it into his lungs. He kicked the trapdoor closed and sprinted for the riverbank where he had stashed his pack.

A shot rang out from behind them and Dylan felt the bullet take him in his right thigh. He yelled and fell to his knees, dropping Felicia. Looking back, he could see Michael at the head of the pack. He withdrew his pistol and fired. Still, Michael and the crowd continued to come. He scooped Felicia back up into his arms and struggled to get his left leg under him in order to rise again. He prayed again for strength. As he heard the crowd behind him growing and drawing closer, he looked up to see how much farther he needed to run and broke into a grin. Pulling up to the bank with guns drawn were five men. They knelt and took aim.

"Don't shoot," he yelled. "Warnings only." Seeing his friends gave him the extra strength he needed and he managed to rise and limp to the waiting boats. "Thanks for showing up, guys. You had me a little worried for a while." They smiled and nodded, firing shots over the crowd's heads. "Police coming?" One of them nodded again. "Let them deal with these people then."

Dylan leaned against the back of the boat and pulled Felicia into his lap, ignoring the pain it caused to his leg from her sitting on it. He